Hats That Fit
A Publication of…

Preface

"This novella exemplifies the timely nobility of five men who, from beneath their ordinary yet distinctive ball caps, helped Joseph Robert Samuels on his life's journey from the 1950s as an eight-year-old Little League baseball player, toward manhood in the 21st century. This veiled semi-autobiography reveals, in simple storytelling narratives, our need for encouragement, self-discipline, healthy relationships, faith and a caring, exemplary father in order to best move ahead during difficult challenges and significant junctures." KRA

"...if anyone cleanses their life from dishonorable things, that person will be a useful vessel, set apart for special purposes, prepared for every good work." (Paraphrase of 2 Timothy

Dedication

Writing a book entails an inordinate amount of quiet time when you must be alone with your thoughts in a peaceful and loving atmosphere. Most would-be authors never have a fighting chance. I am very fortunate to have had a wonderful, highly accomplished, gracious and beautiful wife and friend always nearby who loves me and is my exemplar of visionary determination and faith. She continually acknowledges that it is the life-changing power of God's grace that is our bond for love and that abiding in the Person of Christ must be foremost in our walk. She is the one I most want to be with, in the ordinary and extraordinary times, in our everyday existences and in our adventurous world travels, in life's ups and downs, in times of agreement and disagreement, in moments of joy and sorrow, all of which help to define and amiably bordered so much of my inspiration for living, loving, serving, and writing.

It has been my honor and privilege to journey with Vicky for nearly 20 years whether it be just walking across the street to visit a neighbor, or by trekking into small Nepali communities in the Himalayan foothills; whether by hiking in national forests that border white villages in southern Spain or by breathing in the rich, lush tropical air of Sumatra; whether by refreshing our souls on deserted island beaches near southern Koh Samui or by taxiing hurriedly between the towering skyscrapers of Dubai; whether by clipping along quietly on high speed electric trains throughout Europe or, especially, by jointly delighting in the warm greetings and embraces of family and friends throughout the USA.

    Wherever, whenever, or for whatever, Vicky is the best for me. Life has been and, I am sure, will continue to be a magnificent and stirring ride with her by my side. I love you Vicky Allen and dedicate to you this book in me that is finally out. Kenny

In order to follow us, or to order a book please go to www.kennyreeseallen.com

Acknowledgements

   I acknowledge and honor Robert and Thelma Allen, my remarkably steadfast parents who provided a superb foundation for my life, filled with love and dedication to family, hard work, sacrificial giving of themselves and unsurpassed adventurous weekends, particularly in my teens on the lakes and rivers of Central Florida.

   My brotherly appreciation goes to Donna Allen Leavengood, my beautiful and inspiring sister and childhood companion who is one of America's great school teachers and a family caregiver who has meant so much, to so many.

   As a father, although residing far away over the past two decades, my heart has been deeply affected for the good by my three children, Amy, Matt and Andy who have settled into wonderful careers and have undertaken family roles and responsibilities with honor. You have meant more to me, and inspired me more than I have ever been able to say. Also, I deeply appreciate my stepson, Vicky's youngest, Nelse, for hanging tough in times of upheaval and moving ahead with us while embodying a spirit of adventure and valor.

   I pay professional tribute to my highly accomplished editor, Joan Phillips, without whom this book would probably have remained in its unpublished, rough draft format in the hard drive of my computer. I believed I could write, and surely did enough of it over the past four decades, but she was the one who stepped forward and graciously offered her editorial gifts and talents to help me with "Hats That Fit."

Also, I offer my deep gratitude to those who have journeyed with me for many years and to others who have briefly passed by for a season; some taught me, some encouraged me, some corrected me, some disciplined me, some supported me, some embraced me, some rebuked me, some forgave me, and some even abandoned me—the latter perhaps so I would be a person of God's persuasion and not man's. The ones most significant to me always loved me.

I acknowledge and recognize those I never knew who went valiantly before me, throughout the ages, into all nations, boldly presenting the gospel and mentoring others along their unique paths of faith.

Mostly, I thank my Lord, Jesus, for proving Himself over and over to be the Sufficient One in every venue of my life, yesterday, today, and forever.

Kenny Reese Allen
2 Peter 1:3

Hats That Fit

Kenny Reese Allen

A Coach

A Sage

An Advocate

A Mentor

A Father

Joan Phillips, editor

A Coach

Eight-year-old Joey's greatest hopes and fears had now converged simultaneously as he stepped into the batter's box as a rookie in the bottom half of the final inning. There were two outs and the scored was tied. It was evident to all participants and spectators that there soon would be a dramatic conclusion to Team Red's first official Little League baseball game. Their team coach was strategically encamped in the third base box, from where he would give coded hand signals and continuous words of encouragement to his players. In the on-deck circle, waiting his turn, was the team's best hitter, rubbing some dirt on his hands and swiping them up and down the bat handle to give it some needed grit. All of Joey's teammates, except one, were standing in front of their dugout bench, leaning forward and gripping the mesh, their hats firmly in place. Destiny appeared—Joey knew that he must get on base so he could bring the team's best hitter to the plate. One of Team Red's players remained seated at the far end of the bench, backing up the team's effort with his head bowed as he drew circles in the dirt with his forefinger. Occasionally he re-tightened his shoelaces, disguising the fact that he was praying.

Of all the spectators in the bleachers, the ones who were most important to Joey were his mom, dad, and sister. Hearing their cheers gave him added determination. It sounded like hundreds rooting for the teams, but, really, there were only about fifty. Some had stayed home, expecting a morning rainstorm to materialize. As dark clouds accumulated, everyone knew that if it did rain, the game would be called, since yesterday's downpour had saturated the field. It could hold no more moisture and the low, worn spots in the field would quickly become tributary-forming puddles with the first raindrops.

Earlier, as he tapped the pocket of his glove with his fist from the edge of his bed, Joey thought how fortunate he was that Coach Mitchell had chosen him to be on his team. He knew part of the reason was that his dad had befriended Coach several months before. Without this meeting, Joey knew that he may have never become interested in playing baseball or any other sport. Baseball was the venue where Joey would break through his shell of caution and insecurity. This caring coach was to be a great asset for the character development of hundreds of young men during the coming years, and this was the beginning season—his first and surely the most memorable.

Love for Baseball

Joseph Robert Samuels was born in 1948 in a small farm town in the Deep South, north of Nashville. His family moved from Tennessee to Florida in 1952 when his dad was thirty-three, his sister was five, and his mother was an age that to this day is secretive.

It was in October 1955 in his second grade classroom, that Joey first heard a crackly radio broadcast of a Major League baseball game. By allowing the boys to break academic routine and listen to the World Series on their transistor radios, the judicious teacher knew it would endear them to her. It gave Joey his first opportunity to experience the excitement of a World Series.

After that game, Joey was at home with his family when his curiosity for baseball piqued during the final game of the Yankees vs Dodgers 1955 World Series. At the end of each half inning, during the commercials, he questioned his dad about the game as he scooted on his elbows and belly closer to the TV screen that displayed the first-ever, color broadcast of a baseball game.

Engaged in the drama, his dad had to step over Joey to fiddle with the tin foil attached to the rabbit ears, trying desperately to gain clearer reception. On the final Series out, Joey admitted to himself that he was a fan of the Brooklyn Dodgers—on the day they clinched their first World Series title.

The following school day, wider, boastful chasms formed between those who were faithful to the Yankee "pinstripes" and the finally vindicated Brooklyn "Dodger Blues." There was no middle ground here if you wanted to be considered a worthy baseball fan in the conversational melees during recess.

Partially due to the camaraderie that Joey developed with these sports-minded schoolmates, he decided that he would learn to play baseball and try out for Little League next spring. He was not sure he could make a team, because he was small for his age and had not yet played in a game, except to race around make-believe bases with his friends.

Joey had the gift of quick leg muscles and lightning speed. He wondered how being swift on the base paths might help him get selected to a minor league team. He worried about having the right kind of coach, one that would encourage him and not belittle him. He was little enough.

Joey didn't think much more about baseball for the next two months until that Tuesday morning in 1955 when the Samuels family opened their Christmas gifts. Joey's final present had been carefully wrapped in Dodger blue paper and when held close, smelled of genuine cowhide. Joey was afraid to hope that it might be a glove, but there it was—a brand new, Raleigh Little League baseball glove. Tucked in the web was a bright white baseball, a rare sight in the neighborhood. It was held in place by one of his own belts. His mom and dad had not forgotten his excitement from the Series, last October.

Later that morning, after the traditional Christmas morning pancake breakfast, he and his dad slipped into the back yard, and even though they stood about 30 feet apart, they could not have been closer as they began tossing the ball back and forth. No matter how fast Joey threw it, his dad would haul it in barehanded, if it was within his reach. At times, the ball would skip off the tip of Joey's glove and hit him, but he persevered beyond the cuts and bruises, as well as his mother's concerned looks from the kitchen window.

Joey's dad, Martin, a strong man with tough, calloused hands from years of physical labor, showed Joey how to capture the ball cleanly in the web. A distinct pocket was being formed in the palm of his glove, since Martin instructed him early to slide the forefinger of his left hand over to join with the middle finger. Joey's throws gained such accuracy that his dad seldom had to chase them down.

Martin loved the baseball-great Stan Musial and showed Joey how "Stan the Man" crouched over the plate with his front shoulder low and coiled, ready for an explosive release. *Maybe*, Joey thought, *he could make a team with some practice.*

At dusk Joey rode through the neighborhood on his bike and saw kids his age playing ball and observed that they were more skilled in athletics than he, demonstrated by their adeptness with a variety of new sports paraphernalia given to them at Christmas. In some sense, Little League tryouts already were on their minds, although, officially, it would be four months before four coaches would hand pick 15 players for each of their teams.

At the end of winter, Martin asked around town about who the Little League coaches might be. He knew that Joey retreated from harshness or overly critical teaching styles; his motive was not to shelter Joey but to protect him from a coach who lacked mentoring savvy. Martin wanted to coach his son's team but his occupation as a long-haul truck driver would prohibit his involvement.

Martin heard from a friend that there was a new teacher at the elementary school who had played college ball upstate. Coincidentally, Martin met the teacher when he stepped into the yard while Martin worked on his ancient lawn mower under a shade tree. Gentlemanly in his approach with a firm handshake, the teacher offered his assistance rewinding the pull chord. The two men hit it off when they learned of their mutual passion for '51 Fords. Martin learned that the teacher, his wife, and infant son moved in a few blocks away. He had recently graduated with a degree in Physical Education. Joey listened to the exchange through his bedroom window.

A week or so later, while Joey was riding his bike with some classmates in their newly formed bike-club, he noticed the new teacher driving his well-polished '51 Ford coupe into the church parking lot. As providence would have it, the new Physical Education teacher would become one of the four baseball coaches for the upcoming Little League season. From then on, he was known and respected as Coach Mitchell.

By spring 1956, the intensive, athletic dramas that centered on the fast-approaching Little League season were being played out in Joey's central Florida neighborhood of baby boomers. Dozens of young minor league hopefuls cruised the streets on their Stingray-style bikes—with banana seats, chrome sissy bars, colorful streamers flowing from shoulder-high handlebar grips—and baseball gloves hanging from their handlebars. The bikers gathered from different blocks, and street groups formed to taunt each other. Without the intervention of strong, adult leadership, trouble would surely brew.

    In the post-WWII baby boomer era, communities developed across the nation that included schools, playgrounds, churches, firehouses, grocery stores, libraries—and just as importantly, Little League ball fields—all within a short distance of family residences like Joey's in College Park. Most elementary-aged boys biked throughout their neighborhoods several times a day, their front rims slightly dented from popping wheelies where the driveways meet the curbs. The headwind generated from high-geared racing filtered through their bristly, flat-topped haircuts that had just enough bees' wax on the front to give it a resilient upward flair.

Some of their less valuable baseball cards flapped against the spokes, louder and louder, as they raced faster and faster. The colorful cardboard noisemakers were temporarily held in place by clothespins from their mothers' laundry basket, at least until the cards shredded like confetti and catapulted into the air or wilted in the rain, settling silently onto the red brick streets. Sometimes the bikers cut across the corner of a neighbor's yard in order to be first at the playground, or to gain a slot in the bike rack at school, or to earn a good seat on a round swivel stool at the drug store soda fountain. Some adults would yell at them; most didn't, but all loved the youthful exuberance they represented.

    At the beginning of ball season, three part-time jobs were made available for men to groom the field. One job was hand-dragging a heavy, meshed sled across the dirt infield. Another was building up the pitcher's mound to the proper height and slope and imbedding a heavy plastic-like, brick-sized block used as a push-off point for pitchers. The third was mowing the outfield, wearing tightly laced, steel-toed work boots that soon would be soiled with Florida sand, black dirt, Georgia red clay, and drippings of leaded gasoline. The mower crisscrossed the outfield grass, cutting it short enough for a baseball to pass through on the roll without much hindrance. The playground offered a sweet aroma from the fresh cut grass mixed with the pungent exhaust fumes from a sputtering four-cycle engine. A dime's worth of gas would last a full hour.

        Defining the boundaries is paramount in all

official sports contests. In baseball, a call for a foul ball is more easily judged because of a wooden-wheeled chalk box rolled over the top of a taught string that reached from home plate to the right and left outfield poles. This marked a three-inch-broad line that gave the umpire and the players distinct visual margins for the field of play. If there was a puff of chalk smoke as the ball struck the line, it was fair.

The ball field was located slightly downhill from and about 150 yards in the back of the highly respected, two-story brick schoolhouse on the south side of Princeton Avenue at Helen Street. From home plate, few had ever hit a ball that far, but when someone did, he had free run of the bases until the ball was thrown home—usually long after the batter celebrated his home run in the dugout with his teammates.

Since Joey was relatively small, he naturally identified with the Brooklyn Dodger shortstop, Pee Wee Reese. Joey was amazed at how seamlessly he pulled off double plays with his second baseman, even against the world champion New York Yankees. He wondered if he would ever be able to do that.

Joey was grateful that his father was willing to help his son and capable of teaching him the basics of hitting, throwing, fielding and pitching. He loved chasing pop-ups and grounders while dodging backyard clotheslines and low-hanging branches of orange trees while keeping his eye on the ball. His dad trained him early to have keen peripheral vision; it was that or break something in his body. He learned responsibility as well, since his father insisted that baseballs, thrown or hit, that end up breaking anything, such as windowpanes or screens, would be replaced by the perpetrators, mowing the victim's yard or trimming shrubs at the rate of 50 cents per hour until the debt was satisfied.

    Not only was Joey being groomed by his dad but also by his contemporaries, as small teams would form in sandlots when the weather began to warm. Interest in baseball would increase this time of year, particularly in this region because some Major League teams and players came to central Florida for spring training.

    The guys who were really serious about making a Little League team vigilantly shaped their gloves by hand, rubbing the pocket with three-in-one oil and placing a tattered baseball in its web, wrapping it tightly with a belt and laying it to rest under their pillow each night. As they slept with their gloves, visions of greatness appeared in their dreams.

The Tryouts

The week before tryouts, Joey and some friends gathered each day after school, sat on their bikes outside the mesh-fenced ball field with their gloves hanging from their handle bars, and carefully studied the field. None of them dared to think about crossing onto the sacred grounds without official permission. They had heard it said that anyone caught sneaking onto the field could be charged with trespassing and hauled off to jail in the caged back seat of a police car.

The first Saturday in April would bring with it the beginning of the Little League tryouts for eight and nine year olds. The following four weekday afternoons, for this week only, the tension-filled auditions ensued as young men displayed their skills in front of eager spectators and the four eagle-eyed coaches. Joey wanted mostly to perform well for the new young coach. His mom and dad believed Coach Mitchell would be a good first coach for any young player.

All who made a team would be given t-shirts and hats, donated by local business sponsors. The uniforms would have to be earned; selection to a team was based on merit, and the players would be chosen because of their skills and know-how, not because they showed up for the tryouts. Some less-capable, less-trained, or less-determined candidates were not chosen because they were not better than or equal to the top 60 who would make the cut. Usually, about 80 boys signed up for tryouts. One long week later, the rosters would be trimmed. On that Saturday morning, there would be elation and disappointment, cheers and tears, hugs and hung heads, and boasting and blaming as the reality of life made its joyous or painful stamp in young men's hearts.

    The players and their families looked forward to the traditional opening day ceremonies that came in June before the first official game. Making the "show" and being in a team uniform was a significant achievement for these young men. During the festivities, a few local officials and appointed dignitaries spoke proudly of the teams to the spectators. A cardboard megaphone was used, as each speaker proclaimed the virtues of Little League and its noble influence on the character of young men. A preacher would pray and then, as the American flag in center field was raised, all stood with hats or a right hand covering hearts, as everyone sang the National Anthem. Cheers rose to crescendo at the song's conclusion—"and the home . . . of the . . . brave." The shout, "Play ball!" signaled the ceremony's end and the game's beginning.

Joey desperately wanted to make the cut but knew that he would have to cash in on his strong suit. Although he wanted to hit it long like Hank Aaron, he did not have the strong wrists. He tried to field and throw like Pee Wee Reese but did not have the range or the strong arm. He desired to pitch like Whitey Ford but had no commanding presence on the mound. He did know that he could run faster than anyone in the neighborhood, and that was where he focused his efforts. For one full month before the tryouts, Joey rose extra early each morning before school, suited up in comfortable shorts, a white t-shirt, his favorite hat, and drew the laces tight on his sneakers. Out the door he went, dashing through the neighborhood for up to an hour, with speed and determination. As he ran, he felt pleasure and wondered what or who it was that gave him that sensation, along with the desire and the foreknowledge to focus on this premier athletic talent. He wondered, *Was it because he wanted to please his father and mother by making the team? Was it to be able to boast about his physical prowess? Or, could it be a divine gift for his use on the base paths? Perhaps time would tell.*

Some candidates who tried valiantly during the weeklong tryouts did not appear on the second Saturday, painfully known as "cut day." They chose to avoid the public roll call, assuming they would not be chosen for a team. A few had to suffer through the indignation of getting the public axe in order to finally be convinced and disappointed that they were not accomplished enough. A small number of those who were cut were asked to be batboys, equipment managers, or scorekeepers if they still wanted to participate.

    Ernie, a close friend of Joey's, did not make the grade, which was no surprise. Afterward, he asked if he could keep score at the official games. Math was his strong suit, and the officials were pleased to take Ernie up on his offer. He had physical limitations that kept him from being in the top 60, but in this and in other similar sports tryouts, Ernie offered to help off the field of play, wherever there was a need. His reputation as a dependable and loyal worker preceded him.

    Joey and his two best friends, who had the means and motivation to practice in the pre-season, made the cut and that was good. But on that same day, they learned that each would be on a different team. Though briefly disappointed, making a team was enough to assuage the pain of summertime separation as they pledged their allegiances to their own teams. The three friends would wear different uniforms at the ceremony in June and on the field of battle for the remaining of the summer. They were excited to learn that, if they performed exceptionally during their minor league stint, they could be drafted into the Little League majors next spring without having to try out again in the minors. Perhaps then they could be teammates.

Those in the Little League "majors" played on the higher ground at the other end of the recreational field. That was where the legends of Little League were shaped, like Ricky, a 12 year-old who, two years earlier, had hit a fastball so far over the head of the outfielders and the fence line, that it rolled up the sidewalk and came to rest against the back entry steps of the historic elementary school. Most thought that he had hit a major league homerun distance. Later, the legendary strike story would grow to such proportion that many would say Ricky flew the ball all the way to the schoolhouse, and it broke the window in the principal's office on the second floor. Furthermore, Ricky was a fireball pitcher. Rumor had it that some major league rookies would visibly tremble their way to the on-deck circle, becoming nauseous and hoping to not vomit. Yet each eventually learned that by repeatedly facing Ricky, the terror vanished even if the strike outs didn't. Facing the enemy emboldened them against future obstacles, for they had stepped into the batter's box against an invisible fastball and learned that success was in bravely competing, not in always hitting the ball, or, Lord willing, getting on base. Most who stood firm and who did not bail out when "Rick the Rocket" let it fly, attained future victories against even greater foes.

    Joey often imagined being on one of those major league Little League teams, stepping to the plate, catching a fastball on the nose and freely circling the bases to the roar of his teammates, his parents, his siblings and his coach. He dreamed of the ball clearing the centerfield fence and rolling to a stop at the base of the sprawling oak tree, where he had gained fame at playing marbles.

    Up until now, his greatest success under that oak tree had been against his saintly grandmother's counsel, since he played "keepsies" with his elementary school buddies before and after school. He was skilled enough to be able to bring home pockets full of "cats-eyes" and "ham and egg" marbles on any given day. Joey and his dad did not consider it to be gambling, like grandma did, but instead to be a wise investment with daily dividends made possible by his practice and digital dexterity.

    Joey credited his dad with his skilled marble-shooting technique. He could squeeze shots off from his armchair in the family room with marked precision, hitting dead center to a "bumby" that was on the carpet three paces away. Yet Joey would trade all of those hundreds of marbles that were stored in mayonnaise jars on the top shelf of his bedroom closet for just one keepsake ball that screamed off his bat at home plate and rolled to a stop under that sprawling tree.

The pressing question for Joey and his mom and dad was, "Who would be Joey's first baseball coach?" Dad knew certainly that a coach could set the tone for Joey becoming a solid team player and inspire him to new heights, or he could dishearten him toward disengagement for any future sports. Since that first conversation in the yard, Martin had met with the future Coach Mitchell several times. He liked his conservative manner and his passion for baseball. Martin felt that Coach wanted his team to trust and respect him and understood that by them following his example, they would gain a head start on manhood. Coach wore military gold-framed flight glasses and wanted to exemplify the "I gotcha covered" assurance that young men need. His clothes were always pressed and clean, and his hair was neatly trimmed. Joey and his dad liked that he was just out of college and had come to town early last July to be part of the community as a youth worker for the recreation department.

Joey overheard the guys talking one day about how Coach was an accomplished college athlete as a shortstop and pitcher. He had played varsity for four years with Stetson University. Joey's closest friends, Barney and Dave, said they went to one of his ball games last year and raved at his sure footedness and team leadership. Plus, he was as a master at running the bases, leading the league in stolen bases and runs scored. Opposing batters feared his fastball and sharply breaking curve that turned hard left and dropped near the plate, like it had fallen off a table. One of the parents said that he incurred a serious sliding injury the latter part of his senior year, when his spikes caught in the hard ground while sliding feet first into home. That misfortune kept him from his impending Major League tryout.   A very slight limp at the knee was occasionally noticeable, usually when it rained. Coach Mitchell was still active in a church softball league, and, even at three-quarter speed, was usually the standout player and the one they could always count on to perform under pressure.

    Joey had watched Coach from a distance last summer, as he threw a few warm-up pitches to some teenagers when the recreation department hosted a four-week summer program. Joey observed how Coach patiently endured his less-than-favorite activities of ping-pong, checker pool, volleyball, and tetherball just so he could be part of his true love, teaching kids numbers in the classroom and baseball on the field.

The faces of the four coaches were veiled on the first day of tryouts, shielded from any subtle expressions of approval or disapproval by their ball caps that were pulled tightly down onto their heads. The coaches had clipboards, emblematic of authority, and could be seen making checkmarks with a yellow school pencil tied by a string to the silver circle of their portable desk. Many spectators were clinging to the fences, knuckles exposed, forgetting that they had been warned of injury from foul tips or errant throws.

The first test would be hitting against a pitcher who had committed beforehand to the assignment of making easy tosses from the mound. Next was fielding trials as a coach hit the ball toward each player. The boys had been given their choice of field position. Each tapped their fists into their gloves as they waited nervously for their moment of truth.

Next came the back and forth throws to a partner, with the coaches instructing them to widen the gap after each throw in order to test arm strength and accuracy. Finally, came base running, meticulously timed by every coach on the department's oversized pocket watch as runners circled the bases.

Of all the disciplines, Joey knew running was his best chance at making a team. He was built low to the ground, had fast-twitch muscles, and was able to make 90-degree turns sharply while maintaining his balance. He did not have to go very far to reach the ground when commanded to slide into a base or home. He could scramble to his feet quickly if he needed to continue running to the next base. He hoped that the coach in the red hat would mark him favorably as he dashed around the bases, just as he had dashed through the neighborhood in his early morning workouts. He was glad that Coach Mitchell had seen him outrun all the competition in the 50-yard dashes at recess this past winter and now he was even faster.

  On one of those days last summer, Coach demonstrated to some of the guys his basketball prowess by sinking more than 50 percent of the long ones—soon to be called three pointers—even with a crosswind on the outdoor court. Once during just a thirty-minute lesson, he showed some of the small guys how to do layups from either side, right or left handed. It was all about which foot you pushed off from and the rhythm of your steps as you neared the hoop. Four years later, Joey would draw from that basketball instruction to make the junior high basketball team, one of only two seventh graders to do so. Even as a short right-hander at just under five feet tall, Joey had the left-handed layup down pat at the age of 12, thanks to Coach.

Joey and his dad were grateful when Coach Mitchell called out, "Joey Samuels" as one of his 15 selectees to be on the American Fire and Casualty minor league team. His two best friends were called onto two other teams, one sponsored by Sealtest Dairy and the other by George Stuart Office Supply. It was here and now that the former inseparableness of their relationships would be tested, at least for the upcoming summer.

The Practices

League officials, consisting of the four coaches, a couple of parents, an umpire, and a Little League administrator, set all game-day rules and schedules. There would be several weeks of practice before the first regular season game. Immediately after being sorted into teams, the new rosters quickly gathered and knelt around each of their coaches who led them to their respective corner of the diamond, home, or first, or second or third. The coaches congratulated them, officially introduced themselves, and announced the practice times.

Coach Mitchell told his team to take care of his mimeographed schedule handout and make sure that it made it to the front of the refrigerator, secured by a very strong magnet, ASAP. He emphasized the importance of being at practice on time and to always notify him in advance if unable to attend. Coach's phone number was also on the sheet and easy to remember, since the phone companies issued only five-digit numbers at the time. The team was reluctant to even consider dialing that number, no matter the circumstances, for they thought it better to just show up at the field on time, no matter what. They already liked him well enough to want to please him.

It seemed fitting that Team Red, at this initial gathering, met at home plate for their first skull session, for that was later to be the very location of a defining moment for Joey, Coach, the team and the community that would happen on a cloudy, rainy Saturday morning a few weeks later.

Coach Mitchell took his turn for practice on the field with his fifteen anxious young men after the others had already scarred the base paths, the mound, the batter's box and the infield with their fervent activities. It was highly unusual that Coach did not begin this first practice with the major disciplines of hitting and fielding and throwing. Instead, he had Team Red running the bases, in a variety of ways: first, they each ran the bases from home plate, circling all the way back to home as fast as they could. Second, Coach had them circle past first, head for second, and then quickly reverse, diving back, hopefully before Coach's throw landed in the glove of a volunteer parent at first. They did the same drill at second base, then third before racing for home. It was like he considered running the bases to be the most important aspect of Little League ball.

Joey could hardly contain himself. Coach was teaching them to listen to his voice as he gave such commands as, "Get back" or "Keep running" or "Slide." In performing for Coach, Joey was deep into his element, demonstrating his greatest expertise, enjoying every stride, every slide, every stop, every go, every turn and every return. The whole team was learning to listen and obey.

On a Tuesday afternoon several weeks later, after a grueling two-hour practice that focused on all the fundamentals of the game, Coach announced that Team Red's first official game would be here soon. He repeated his standard, "Rain or shine, always come to the field on time, dressed out and ready." They knew what dressed out meant, since up until now, everyone had fitted themselves in tightly laced sneakers, protective blue jeans, a clean T-shirt, and a favorite baseball hat. Joey's choice hat was Dodger blue.

Coach Mitchell led the the team into the parking lot near his pristine '51 Ford, opened the trunk and lifted out a large, sealed cardboard box. It was like Christmas morning. The team sensed that this had to be the "dressed out" part of his request. The outside of the box had a label that read:

    From: Pickerill's Sporting Goods
    Edgewater Drive

    To: Coach Mitchell
    American Fire and Casualty Team
    Princeton Elementary School

The team crowded close, making their best effort to get as near to the trunk as possible without being pushy. Coach pulled out his small but sharply honed Swiss army knife and cut the duct tape wrapping. He pulled two bright red items from two smaller boxes. Beaming with approval, Coach took a deep breath and introduced the team to their new uniforms. He proudly held up for all to see a plain red T-shirt and a red hat with the three white block letters, AFC. Coach then curled the brim of one of the hats and pulled it firmly onto his brow. He said that these hats symbolized battle helmets on the ball field. He emphasized taking care of them, informing the team that this local insurance office donated the uniforms and that every player would be expected to drop by their place of business on Edgewater Drive to thank the office manager, pledging to wear both items respectfully and proudly on and off the field.

    The T-shirts varied slightly in size, with a few extras in case there were special circumstances ahead for honoring others or replacing ones that could no longer be made clean by mom's hand scrubbing. The hats were all the same size with a five-hole, adjustable plastic strap in the back. Coach said, "These all need to be shaped and fitted; I'll help you."

    He instructed them to remove their old hats and watch him closely as he demonstrated how to "curl" the brim, in order to look the part of a serious ballplayer. It had to be molded into a semi-U-shape and allowed to spring back, then rolled with both hands until the edges were about 30 degrees short of perpendicular to the ground. Coach said, "No "squaring" allowed; that was too "showy." It took a very special touch to do it right, and Coach had to give the final nod of approval before they could put them on, officially. He showed them how to pull them on their heads from front to back, then pull down near the back strap, while securing the brim firmly, straight ahead and slightly down. After completion, Coach beamed, "Now those are some fine looking baseball hats!"

During Team Red practices, the boys always were eager to show their individual prowess, and were told they knew that in due time that would come, meanwhile they were growing in the grace and knowledge of a team effort. Coach held firmly to his mission of a carefully orchestrated plan, centered around base-running skills.

Sometimes Coach would have the team come to the field and sit with him on a barren area outside the center field fence under the oak tree. From there he would comment on the strengths and weaknesses of the other team that was practicing. He spoke objectively, never belittling their future opponents. Coach asked each of his team members to include a type of mathematical hierarchy from one to ten to assess each opponent's throwing, fielding, and running abilities. He said, "Be careful not to tell anyone, except your parents, about our preparations."

To keep his instruction on a personal level, he also taught individually, dropping on one knee, peering into young eyes, speaking softly yet firmly, while giving a particular offensive or defensive tactic that fit their athletic capability. He encouraged his young charges to freely come to him with any questions or concerns about baseball.

At the end of all practices, Coach said, "Now, let's run the bases." They knew what that meant. The sequence was first to circle the bases all the way back to home and slide in, running along one base length behind the other; and then, after the team caught it's breath, each would run past first and dive back; run past second and dive back; run past third and dive back; run from third to home and choose a favorite type of slide, maneuvering to try to avoid an imaginary tag from their awaiting coach.

The team was jelling together into a unique style of Little League ball, working hard to solidify their team spirit by never grumbling about all the work. With the help of a few young team leaders, they cheered each other on to run faster, jump back quicker, and slide harder, believing they would compete best by becoming preeminent in running the bases. Joey was becoming one who led the others.

From the beginning, Coach confirmed his teamwork strategy as he revealed his thoughts on winning Little League games. He often said, "In the minors, games are usually won or lost not with the single, hefty base-clearing swing of a mighty bat. Instead, it comes down to who is smarter and quicker on the base paths."

This was a stroke of genius among the kids, but not with all the parents. A few grumbled and complained to Coach about how strange it seemed to do this repeated running and so little hitting, pitching, fielding and throwing. Actually, Coach spent a great deal of time on all aspects of the game. It was just that most parents arrived near the end of the practices and would see only the base-running sessions at the conclusion of each practice. Coach understood and was kind, yet remained undeterred in his primary mission for Team Red.
    Joey still wanted so much to hit home runs, but Coach told him that Hank Aaron's ability to hit the long ball was due to the strength and speed of his enormous wrists. Coach demonstrated for Joey how to turn into the pitch with the strength and speed of his legs and hips, which would result in success. Otherwise, Joey would be no threat at the plate. Also, each player was given verbal queries, where they had to anticipate what they would do with a batted ball that came their way. Eventually, they learned that while on the field, they must be mentally alert to all options that would have to be chosen at the crack of a bat.
    Team Red players became particularly confident that, when it came to base running, they knew far more than the other three teams combined. Coach insisted that they needed to

remain humble when they began to win their games, otherwise they would be tripped up by pride. Also, he instructed them to be gracious in defeat, congratulating the victors—an extra-mile philosophy that Coach believed would make the difference between good, better, and best. He drew people near with his kind and friendly ways, not with a harsh, authoritarian mantle.

The team learned that when there were two or more teammates on the base paths, one could draw a throw his way in order that his teammate could advance. Self-sacrifice was taught as a necessary ingredient for the good of the team. Therefore, all were taught to lay down a bunt when he gave the signal from third. Every player learned how to wait until the last second to square off to bunt so the defense would be caught off guard. Sometimes they would fake it and quickly re-square in time to swing fully at the pitch. Key signals for any type of play came from the third base coach's box. Missed signals were discussed later, in private, and never with public ridicule.

Team Red would soon be well-known for their daring maneuvers and near disastrous tag outs, and sometimes for looking foolish, as their bold attempts occasionally ended in embarrassing outs. Many runs would cross home plate; many more would be stopped short with a good defensive maneuver. Coach taught each of his players the importance of ruffling the feathers of the opponents but never by taunting them. He said that there was always plenty of room within sportsmanship and humility to win.

After enduring many late-afternoon, midweek practices, Team Red trusted that Coach knew what he was doing. They were taught repeatedly to keep an ear tuned for Coach's voice above all others and follow his commands. As a pre-emptive caution, he spent valuable time instructing each of his players how to slide safely in order to avoid injury. There were several different styles of sliding: hooking one leg under the other, going in feet first on your back, diving in head first on your belly, going in on one side or the other, or anything that safely worked.

Unusual, and even controversial, was the way that Coach would toss the ball in the air at home plate and bat it straight toward his own base runners. Initially, they were afraid but quickly learned to dodge them and keep running. Coach insisted that they have their batting helmets on when at bat or when running the bases, or even in the on-deck circle. They looked like unfashionable, cold weather, plastic earmuffs. Sometimes, they would lose their helmets and hats while racing around the bases, and Coach would yell, "Keep running! Don't go back!" Sometimes, the ball would hit a player in the base path and Coach would holler, "Are you OK?" And then follow up with, "You're outta there!" That was the rule of baseball; get hit by a struck ball while in the act of reaching a base, and you are out.

    Team Red met together around the neighborhood while underneath their red caps, whether they were riding their bikes, having a cherry coke in a Hum-Dinger cup at the local drug store fountain, or playing on the schoolyard. Coach encouraged them in team meetings, "This cap is your trophy, and it is like a battle helmet. Wear it proudly. Along the way, they were learning to be dedicated fans, usually watching Saturday Major League games on their black and white TVs, especially if their dads were home.

    Days seemed to crawl by as they practiced harder and harder, anticipating their first official game. In a way, they were multi-tasking, learning to be knowledgeable about the rules and etiquette of this sport, while being skilled participants on the field and good citizens off. Coach stayed in contact with all their school teachers, and if they fell behind in their work, or their grades dropped low, he would bench them the very next practice. No one ever faltered more than once. They became very close to Coach, because they trusted him and knew that he cared deeply for them. Occasionally he would stop by their homes and say hello to their families as he walked the neighborhood with is wife and son. Ultimately, Coach wanted them to be leaders, not followers. They began to sense the local influence of being on a team that was building an honorable reputation. A higher kind of life was unfolding before them, one that Coach was emulating with every word and deed.

The Big Day

Finally, after a Monday practice, Coach said the words Team Red players had eagerly awaited, "So, this Saturday is our first official game. Come on time. Be there by 10 am, sharp. Wear your uniform proudly, and be ready to run some bases." They were excited and confident to be on a well-prepared team that had a distinctive style of baseball to deliver to the community. Coach told them this before they headed home from their final practice. "Guys, something very special is in store for us at this first game. I just know it."

It rained most of Friday and some of the minor-leaguers pedaled by the low end of the playground to take a look. Droplets fell from their ball caps onto their noses and muddy water striped the backs of their T-shirts from their two-wheeled pathways into the puddles near the curbs. The four teams may have had different color hats, but all minor league team members were alike, since they all wanted the same thing—that Saturday's game would not be washed out. They were all concerned that small rivers would flow down from the higher ground near the oak tree and onto the outfield grass. Eventually, water would settle into the low areas at second base. Underground tributaries proceeded from there to home plate and the white octagon would be covered with slippery sludge. The young men who were digging in for a chance to hit a home run in practices had left the deepest wounds in the area of the batter's box. If it would just stop raining soon, the field crew could repair the field of play. The boys hated to think that they might have to go back home in the rain on Saturday before they got their first chance to officially run the bases. No matter what, they would be at the field long before game time.

    Despite a drizzle that continued until midnight, many players would arrive early on Saturday, some even by 8 am. Joey was the first one there. Even though the sun had broken through and evaporation had begun, the dirt and clay infield was a darker shade than usual. Some shallow puddles still remained, but thankfully they were being rapidly diminished, minute-by-minute, as if some type of celestial, silent, invisible vacuum had begun sweeping over the field.

    The same workers as before, including Coach, were putting the final touches on this athletic theatre. The field's symmetry was destined to be, even if playing ball was denied. Groomers displayed unwavering hope as they carefully executed their tasks like professionals laying the boundaries from home to the outfield pole, squaring off the batter's boxes, and succinctly marking the third and first base coach's areas. Then there were the on-deck circles, which would have a defined circumference for the nervous, kneeling young men preparing to face the enemy—hoping, even praying, that they could make solid contact. Even a walk or a sacrificial bunt would we be a victory, particularly for Team Red.

    One blue-capped, high-school-aged young man and two rookie coaches stood around home plate discussing the situation, occasionally glancing skyward. At least their shoes had not sunk into any mud. One man represented Team Orange, the opposing team; one represented Team Red; and one represented baseball's on-the-field authority. The coaches showed respect to the young umpire from the opening handshake, for they knew that he had that extra measure of expertise that had come with six weeks of after-school umpire training and years of participation in this sport, much of it on this very field.

"Blue" demonstrated his wisdom by telling the coaches of his desire to keep the game moving by applying an expanded strike zone for the young pitchers. Otherwise, there would be too many walks and not enough hitters swinging the bat. Coach Mitchell said that his Team Red would not be challenging any of his judgment calls. The only time he would get involved would be if it related to the rules of the game. The Team Orange coach agreed and nodded his head.

The players on Team Red had been taught that they needed to be respectful of "Blue," who was easily recognizable with trademark azure headgear and matching T-shirt fit tightly over his padded sternum. Unlike the players' hats, his had an unusually short brim that allowed him to place his steel barred mask over his face, thus protecting his face from foul tips, wayward pitches, or flying bats slung behind by eager batters propelling themselves forward out of the batter's box. Team Red was taught that for every action, there is an equal and opposite reaction, putting any young hitter in danger of harming someone near the plate if they tossed their bats behind them.

The tension of the pre-game moments brought one of the guys sitting at the end of the

Team Red bench to a moment of reflection and numinous pause. He reached down toward the ground, scratched in the dirt and fiddled with his shoelaces, yet his lips were moving reverently and his eyes were closed. His name was Tony. Finally, a decision was made. If the rain held off, the game would start at 10 a.m. as planned. The good news spread quickly. The game would go forward provided the rain held off.

    The volunteer scorekeeper, Ernie, began to draw a simple spreadsheet on the scoreboard with white chalk. He was the first to sense the decision by "Blue" and began designing the inning-by-inning markers. Soon all knew of the vote as both coaches raced back toward their home dugouts. Players and coaches put their game faces on as they adjusted their hats, pulling them tightly in place for the battle ahead. "Blue" maintained his stoic composure in order to exemplify his authority, reproving that he was an in-charge, rule-centered ump, not to be swayed from justice by emotion. Inside, he was nervous, since this was his first game as an officiator.

    It seemed possible that the heavens would stay closed, as if God was giving His nod of approval. Thankfully, not even a sprinkle appeared the next thirty minutes as each squad took the field for their pre-game warm-ups. One team was very attentive toward analyzing the strengths and weaknesses of those throwing the ball around. The other team seemed to be more driven by wanting to get to the plate in order to take hefty swings at trying to hit the long ball. All on Team Orange would be offered just three pitches at the plate from their coach as their leader lobbed his throws in like softball tosses in order to build their confidence.

When it was Team Red's turn to bat, they demonstrated that they marched to the beat of a different drummer, readied for play by refusing their opportunity to practice their hitting and fielding. Instead, they exchanged that time for running back and forth near the outfield fence in a predetermined running exercise, perplexing to most onlookers. This exercise and warm-up was merited in light of Coach's plan to center on Team Red's mission, as well as a calculated move to unnerve the other team. Even the parents of Team Red thought it odd, and some dropped their gaze downward in embarrassment or rolled their eyes as a display of, "What is this guy doing?'

The teams and coaches came back to their respective dugouts and "Blue" waited for the next sequence of events. The major league side of the field led the opening day traditional ceremony as people on that end of the playground respectfully stood and removed their ball caps. The minor league side followed suit. A man in a short-sleeved dress shirt with a dark tie appeared at home plate, wearing pressed slacks and shiny dark shoes. He was from the local Baptist church and began to pray, out loud. Everyone seemed to respect what he said and all eyes were opened after he closed with, "In Jesus' name." This prayer was meant to secure the blessings of God and the aspirations of all attending. Then, everyone placed their right hand, or hat, over their heart as they sang the National Anthem, the "Star Spangled Banner." After the closing stanza, ". . . and the home of the brave," the major league umpire shouted with right hand raised, "Play Ball!" The minor league ump did the same on his end of the playground.

The two "Blues" began putting on their facial armor and tightening the straps behind their heads. They grabbed a small whiskbroom that had been secured by a special belt loop in the back of their trousers and leaned over home plate, sweeping the plate clean. They rubbed the three official baseballs to be used in their respective games. The two extras were stuffed in a pocket at the front of their vests as they waited for time to reach 10:00. Umpire school had taught them well.

Knowing that only three balls were budgeted for each game, eager fans readied themselves to run after strays, since all spheres that landed beyond the fences would need to be quickly chased down and returned. These speedsters would later be honored with a free cold drink after the game. For them, it was a badge of honor to just be able to win the race to the ball and then toss it back over the fence. It was their charitable contribution to the preservation of the game. No one kept the ball for himself.

  Team Red players encircled their coach, who knelt on one knee outside the dugout, positioning himself for his final instructions. They quieted the very moment that Coach removed his hat and they all solemnly bowed their heads. Coach Mitchell then prayed, "Lord, please protect these young men and help them to put forth their best effort. May we be humble in victory or gracious in defeat. Thank you for providing this time without rain. Amen." As all hats were replaced, Tony glanced skyward and smiled. He was not on the starting nine but knew he had a key role to play.

  Coach reached for the nearby, 26-inch team bat and held it vertically in front of the players as they rose from their kneeling positions. They each placed one hand above another's until all 16 right hands had a firm grip. Coach's free hand firmly covered the top knob. He gave the signal, "1…2…3," and they shouted in unison as they broke from the huddle, "Let's run some bases!" It was quite an auspicious occasion for Team Red.

One by one, Team Red players tugged downward on the brims of their hats while racing to their positions on the field. Nine of them ran bravely toward frontline duty onto a field that had been prepared in advance for them, determined to skillfully and valiantly defend the bases against all intruders, especially home. Coach had chosen only eight-year-olds for his team, so this would be their first officially sanctioned baseball game. Were it not for the tight-fitting hats, nine sweaty brows would have been revealed.

During their first defensive encounter in the top half of the first inning, Team Red was more appreciative than ever that Coach had taught them both individual effort and team trust. They held the opponent, GS Office Supply's Team Orange, to only three runs, in spite of four walks given up by their pitcher. Generally, they functioned well as a team, although as tense young men participating in the first inning of their first game, there were some mental and physical mistakes. Most rewarding to Coach was that they had picked off two base runners that had tried to go too far. None on the American Fire players were down on each other when their errors occurred or when four ball fours were called by Blue: Coach had taught the power of encouragement instead of the ill results of disheartening blame.

As they ran off the field, at the end of the top half of the first inning, they could hardly wait to execute their offensive base-running strategies. They felt it could come down to which team got the most runners on base and who ran the bases the best. They were confident it would be them. They remembered what Coach had taught them about offense, "When you have your turn at bat, be patient and find a way to get on base. Walks are good, but swing hard if you get a good pitch. Look for my hand signals. Listen for my voice."

The team appreciated that Coach Mitchell was always at his post in the third base coaching box when they were up to bat. He was their key, especially when the heat was on. They liked the simple geometry of being able to see him while dashing from base to base and knowing they had a trusted voice they could hear when heading for home.

In their first at-bat, "Team Red" scored four runs with the help of two hits, three errors, and five walks. Three runs came because they had run the bases with calculated recklessness as the other team made some expected misjudgments. The only independently scored run was when Jimmy hit a fastball, at least faster than most, that reached all the way to the left center field fence on the roll. He never let up as he listened to Coach, circling the bases and sliding into home just under the tag. He beamed like never before. It was his first official Little League hit, and it was a particularly significant moment, since it would be the first time the whole team had a chance to exuberantly welcome a teammate at home plate. There were two interested assistant coaches from the Little League majors in the stands who were already sizing up Jimmy for a possible bye next spring in order to bring him straight into the majors.

The lead bounced back and forth. Simultaneously, the ominous rain clouds began to accumulate. Through the completion of four innings, Team Red's opponent had the lead, 9 to 8. By the time Joey came up for his third at bat in the bottom half of fifth inning, with two outs, the score was tied at 12—12. GS Office Supply had scored three runs in their top half of the fifth, giving them a temporary four-run lead before the bottom half of the inning began. Team Red came back strong and had already scored four runs in their bottom half with one out still to go. Joey would soon be in the batter's box.

When added to the inevitability of the fast approaching rain clouds, the score on the chalky scoreboard beyond the backstop made it clear that the end was near. It would be brought about by one of three scenarios: one more run scored for victory, a third out, or the rain.

Everyone trusted that Ernie had accurately maintained the correct score. In spite of not making a team, Ernie loved the game and could talk baseball stats, strategies, and name all of the famous players with the best of baseball historians. By the time he was seven, Ernie had developed into a good athlete. This was no longer true, but he was glad he could continue to give himself for the good of this game and did what he could to help his friends and the community. He was a fast friend of Joey's and kept secret from the other teams the unique plan that he knew Coach was implementing. He liked Coach's style.

Just before Joey stepped into the batter's box, he remembered what Coach had whispered to him in the on-deck circle just a moment before. "Joey, hit the first pitch you can reach. The first pitch you can reach." Joey understood. The pitcher nervously threw the first one too high and too wide for Joey to even consider. The next pitch was better, within reach. When he swung, he made contact, but since it was so low, he could only "top" it.

The ball rolled weakly toward the third baseman, inching slowly toward the foul line. It trickled to a stop just short of the chalky third base line. The ball was picked up by the pitcher, who reached it just before the charging third baseman arrived. From habit, the pitcher took a quick wind up before he threw it toward the first baseman. Joey had seen him do this before in one of his practices and knew he had a good chance to reach first. That thought caused the adrenaline to pump, and Joey added to that his physical quickness. He had it in high gear by the time he neared first base. During his 60-foot run down the baseline, he could not help but think about heading for second should the first baseman bobble the throw. But he knew what was most important was that he arrived safely. He listened all the way down the line for Coach's voice. All he heard was, "Run Joey. Run."

    The umpire had to make this call without help, since the other ninth-grade volunteer umpire held his position near second base. "Blue" raced toward first, just outside the baseline, a few steps behind Joey. He listened for the sound of the ball hitting the first baseman's glove versus Joey's foot stomping the bag. The foot was first by a split second, and Blue yelled, "Safe!" He quickly crisscrossed his arms below his waist twice with his mask still in one hand. Blue's final word, and his accompanying motions signaled great news for Joey, for Coach Mitchell, for mom and dad, for sis, for Team Red, and for one half of spectators. The game was still on.

Joey made a ninety-degree turn to the right and semi-circled back to first. Coach had been firmly commanding him shortly after he arrived, "Stay, Joey, stay." He clung to the canvas bag with his clenched toes inside his sneakers turned downward. He knew that Coach's word was law and was also good for him and for the team. He was thankful to have Coach's clear instruction at such a critical moment.

He basked in the glory of his first official Little League hit, knowing that he and his team now had a chance to score the winning run. He was abruptly awakened from his moment of euphoria when he heard both coaches call for "timeouts." His first thought was, "Lord, please don't let it rain now." The opposing coach hurried to the mound to talk with his pitcher, as the infielders and the catcher attentively gathered around. He spoke his plan to Team Orange and then jogged back to their dugout.

When the catcher returned to his position, Coach Mitchell had already begun his short chat with his next batter, Charlie, who was a good hitter. If need be, Charlie could smack it on the ground or drop a bunt in any direction requested. Few had ever seen him swing and miss a pitch. The opposing catcher faintly heard the whispered instructions to Charlie as Coach said, "Charlie, hit the first pitch you can reach toward the second baseman on the ground. Get to first safely and help Joey get around second and on to home." Charlie's eyes gleamed as he nodded and reached down to grab some dirt, first for his sweaty hands, then for the bat handle. He thought about spitting but held back because he knew his mom was in a front row bleacher seat. Joey suspected that Coach had actually wanted the catcher to hear some of his instructions to Charlie.

  Team Red's rumored fame for expertly running bases was ready for reality. The catcher, like a spy who had secretly gathered enemy plans, raced to the pitcher's mound. He motioned the infielders to gather around him. He told them what he had heard Coach say to Charlie. The second baseman was the one most affected by the news and even more nervous than before with the anticipation of a grounder that could soon come his way. Meanwhile at the plate, Charlie was already thinking about how he could draw a throw toward himself as he feigned his way toward second and dove back quickly and safely in order for Joey to circle the bases and make it home.

  By then, Coach had trotted up to Joey at first base, knowing that time was of the essence as the clouds darkened. He leaned over to whisper instructions to Joey. No one but Joey would hear him. Coach disguised his words by pulling off his hat and using it to visually shield his lip movements from all spying eyes.

Coach instructed, "Joey, let's win this game now." Joey could hardly wait for the battle plan as Coach continued, "When Charlie hits the ball toward the second baseman on the ground, run as fast as you can, but keep an eye out for the ball. Do not ease up. Push hard off second base as you dig for third. Listen for my voice, and you will know what to do."

Joey pictured the plan in his mind. He thought how gutsy this was, though it would not be until later that he and others would learn the pure genius of Coach's plan. Joey knew that with the ball going to the second baseman off of Charlie's bat, and with him not letting up but pounding ahead for third, some fielding and throwing errors could be expected. Plus, loud shouts and differing instructions would be coming from everyone who was for or against either team. Hollers would come from infielders and outfielders, from fans and from foes, from both coaches and from all directions. Joey knew to listen to but one voice—that of his trusted Coach. All he had to do was run fast, avoid the bounding ball, and follow Coach's instructions.

To add to the drama, rain clouds darkened the sky but still no drops. Joey's thoughts rebounded briefly to when his teammate, Tony, had prayed quietly just before the game began. He also remembered Coach saying that he was thankful to God for this time without rain. Joey wondered, "Could the heavens be holding back the rain for such a defining moment as this?" It was the first time he had ever uttered a heartfelt divine request; albeit silent, his prayer was sincere. *Lord, please help us do our best*, he thought.

As Charlie shuffled his sneakers into a firm position in the batter's box, Joey remained in full contact with the inside edge of the first base bag with his left foot. He leaned toward second with his right foot forward and extended his right arm, ready to sling it backward for some jet-like propulsion, like Coach had taught. Joey knew that if he left too soon, the game would be over when Blue called, "Out!" since leading off the base was against Little League rules. The runner must wait until the ball crosses home plate or is hit before he can leave the bag. He was watching and listening as Charlie's bat made contact. Joey knew he must remain mentally engaged and run like the wind. He knew it would be easy to become distracted. The "final play" was on and his ears were fine tuned for one voice.

The scorekeeper seemed to show particularly special interest as he put away his chalk and reached for his crutches. With help strapped to his wrists and more resting underneath his armpits, he was able to stand and see. Loyal fans of Team Red knew that the real action had just begun. Spectators, remembering the boys in red who had focused on running practice while playing ball in back yards, sandlots, and traffic-free streets, stood in anticipation of the next few seconds.

Joey swung his right arm backward, thrust his left leg forward and bolted forward with all his might a millisecond after Charlie had hit the ball. He glanced quickly at the bouncing ball now heading his way. On a dead run, he leaped over the grounder and rocketed toward second, grazed the base with his right foot, pushed off firmly on a dead run, headed pell-mell for third and, hopefully, beyond. He listened for Coach's voice. Only in the distant background was he aware that many other voices were screaming deliriously. He clearly heard coach yell, "Run the bases, Joey."

Half way to third base his earmuff helmet fell off. Coach instantly commanded with the authority of a battle-trained officer, "Keep running, Joey. Don't go back. Go for home!"

Toeing the inside corner of the third base, Joey turned for home. His peripheral vision eyeballed an unprotected portion of the plate. He was three strides past third base when suddenly his treasured red hat flew off his head, landing behind him just outside the baseline.

Charlie's grounder had been mishandled by the second baseman, slipping beneath his glove, proceeding through his legs and rolling into the freshly mowed outfield grass. The right fielder charged the loose ball and retrieved it with his bare hand. Charlie was rounding first, and, as planned, he lured the outfielder into throwing the ball toward him at first base. The opposing players thought they could get Joey out. Had the outfielder thrown the ball to the pitcher on the mound, the play would have been over, and Joey would have been stopped at third base.

The tag at first was unsuccessful as Charlie dove headfirst back to the bag just in the nick of time. He was called safe by the other ump. "Blue" held his position at home, knowing that Joey was headed his way. Charlie jumped to his feet and considered bolting for second. Judging how close Joey was to home, Charlie remained at first. The results were now out of his hands, and he proudly knew that he had played his part without need to be overly heroic.

After his late tag on Charlie, the first baseman whirled counter-clockwise and fired a belt-high bullet toward the catcher. Joey had hesitated only a split second when his hat flew off and had regained his momentum. Relying on Coach's final instruction to go for home, Joey was nearly there when he heard Coach yell "Slide, Joey! Slide!"

Joey could see that vulnerable portion of home plate. Could he squeeze in there? What kind of slide should he choose? Joey's eyes widened with anticipation as his center of gravity shifted forward. He knew that he was within just a few feet of a Team Red victory or, dare he think, a personal defeat.

He lunged forward, diving with all his remaining strength. Now he was flying, headfirst, stretched out in the air, face down, anticipating a soon and certain awkward landing somewhere near the catcher's feet. He wasn't concerned in style points, just results. He landed on his belly and slid slid through the chalk-marked batter's box, crashing into the kneeling catcher's body block. Feet and arms flailed as dozens of anxious gasps were released from outside the mesh fence. Joey's left hand touched home. He waited for the call, which seemed to take an eternity. Joey was spent.

Blue had strategically positioned himself just over the catchers' left shoulder for the best possible view. He knew this call would be his first game-ending decision and justice must prevail. The first baseman had transformed a weak throw from the right fielder into a missile that tracked straight and true. The catcher caught the ball with his bare right hand, swirled to his left and reached down to make a tag. Everyone knew it had to be close. There was no doubt of that. Blue knew the results before anyone else.

    The vociferous call came from Blue, as he tore off his steel mask and hollered loud enough for all to hear, "You're Out!" At that same instant, Blue thrust his right thumb skyward. This would be his final call no matter who might agree or disagree. He was well trained and ready for any who might want to argue the call. It was the right call. Even though Joey was dazed from the collision, he accepted that Blue was right and so did both coaches.

    A lesson that had been building from day one, for all there to witness would now be manifested. Little did Joey know that he was about to be proclaimed a valiant soldier on the field of battle who had given his all. In the instant after he was pronounced out, his thoughts bounced from one side of his brain to the other and his emotions from one side of his soul to the other. *"Maybe I could have run faster?" "Why did I have to hesitate as my hat flew off? "I was so close." "What will the team say?" "How will Coach Mitchell react?" "Will some people be angry and argue against the call?" "Did Mom, and Dad, and Sis see how hard I tried and how fast I ran those bases?" "Will my teammates blame me?"*

While spitting wet dirt and wiping chalk dust away from his uncovered forehead, Joey, still in a daze, rolled over on his back. The first person he was able to recognize was Coach Mitchell. In his lifetime he would never forget Coach's facial expression and astonishing words. Coach dropped to his knees, leaned in toward Joey's face, and exclaimed so all would know, "Atta boy Joey! What a great run! Man, that slide was perfect! I knew you could do it! I am so proud of you. Man, did you ever run those bases!"

Soon, the whole team was following Coach's lead as they began whooping and hollering. The other team and its coaches were just as ecstatic as the Team Orange defensive team ran off the field toward the pandemonium at home plate. Joey heard exclamations from his teammates such as, "What a game!" "Atta boy, Joey!" "Did you see the way Joey jumped over that grounder, and how Charlie dove back into first?" And on it went. The opponents reiterated praise toward all their teammates as well, "What an awesome throw!" "Great catch!" "Way to play it!" "Man, what a great tag! What a game!"

It was then that Joey realized that his red hat was still behind him, somewhere. He sat up just in time to see Coach Mitchell hurry away from home plate, down the third base line, scoop up a red hat, shape it, tap the dirt off onto his jeans, and present it proudly back to Joey, who was now sitting cross-legged, wide eyed, and smiling in the batter's box. Coach reached down to Joey and said, "Here's your helmet, soldier." And with that, the beaming coach extended his hand to help Joey to his feet.

Many eyes shifted toward Ernie's chalk scoreboard. The game was a tie though one would never know it from the cheering of both sides. Suddenly, a lightning bolt far enough away to present no threat of striking anywhere in College Park pierced the sky, accompanied by thunder a few seconds later as the heavens opened to a steady drizzle onto the field, a typical seasonal outpouring of Florida's liquid sunshine. Laughter overtook the players and spectators alike. Joey had already pulled his hat firmly onto his head when he looked heavenward into the rain and acknowledged this moment with the tip of his hat.

Coach turned away from home plate and walked briskly toward Team Orange's celebration just outside their dugout. As he neared the catcher and the first baseman Coach said, "What a terrific throw and play at the plate. Congratulations!"

Turning toward the team he said, "All of you played an outstanding game!" He then offered his right hand to their coach and said, "Great job, coach." There was a firm handshake in return. Nearby, several proud dads stood by, waiting to shake hands with both coaches.

Leaning against the mesh fence in the background was "Blue." He looked relieved. Coach acknowledged him with, "Good job, young man. You made a speedy and courageous call, and it was the right one. Congratulations."

Both teams retreated to their dugouts, although, without a roof, they offered no shelter from the rain. With their many friends and family surrounding them, both Team Orange and Team Red basked in their victory. Just as quickly as the rain appeared, it disappeared. Baskets of food and coolers full of soda were brought from car trunks to their respective areas.

Before Coach came to the dugout to celebrate, he marched briskly toward the score-keeping area to thank Ernie, who was re-posting the final tally since the rain had blurred and streaked some of his calculations. Ernie seemed content, knowing he had been a part of something that would never be fully erased. His fresh marks on the board articulated the game's story.

Innings	1	2	3	4	5	Total
George Stuart Office Supply	3	2	2	2	3 -	12
American Fire & Casualty	4	2	1	1	4 -	12

    Although Ernie had never qualified for an official team, his team effort shined. Bearing life with the weight of his crutches and leg braces, he brought light upon his determination and noble character. Polio restricted his performance on the field, yet off the field, he was an exemplary and much needed team player. Disease may have invaded his body three years ago, but he bravely persevered. Even in life's difficulties, he pressed forward valiantly, participating when and where others may have given up.

    Most knew what Coach must be saying to Ernie, face to face through the backstop fence, because the young scorekeeper, without hesitation, made his way toward the Team Red dugout—crutches, leg braces, pain, smiles, and all. He proudly sat down on the bench next to Tony, relishing together their part in the team victories.

    Coach reached for the equipment bag and pulled out a fresh red hat and placed it on Ernie's head. The properly sized T-shirt shortly followed. Coach spoke loudly enough for all to hear, "Ernie, would you like to be the equipment manager and assistant coach for the best base-running team in

Little League history?" Thus, for the rest of the season, Ernie served Coach and the team by being well prepared for every game and practice, never complaining but always encouraging his teammates. The bats, balls, catcher's mask, and earmuff helmets always were perfectly lined inside the dugout, just like Coach instructed. Ernie passed his scorekeeping duties on to another young man who had not officially made a team.

The day after that first game, Ernie's parents went to Peterson's Sporting Goods, where they purchased four more identical red hats for themselves and their other two younger children, paying extra to have the letters AFC heat-pressed onto the crest. They also stopped by the local AFC insurance office to thank the manager for his sponsorship of such a spirited and well-coached team.

No one at the field wanted to leave; the moms continued to hand out an abundance of cold drinks and hot dogs with heaping scoops of homemade potato salad weighing down the side of the paper plates. Coach's wife, with infant Billy in tow, helped serve everyone. All had won. Or was it a tie? The fathers stood near their sons, with pride. Joey's dad, mom, and sister were in the thick of the celebration, wearing their red T-shirts and hats that they had purchased the day after Coach handed them out to Team Red a few weeks earlier.

Families, players, and fans picked up the debris and began heading for home as a recurring light rain signified the end of the festivities. Biking together, the boys from both teams headed to the corner drug store that made the delicious, gigantic carbonated cokes with real syrup for only twenty cents. Game news had spread, and the store owner congratulated the victors and give them all free refills.

When Joey arrived home, he toweled off his face in the garage, hung his hat on the rack among all of his dad's collectible coverings, and went inside to take a warm shower. He was especially thankful that his dad had driven his long-haul, refrigerated truck all night from New York City to be at the game. He couldn't be in the stands for them all, but Dad always tried to be there, and Joey knew that.

Joey's mom and dad were discussing the Coach's significant impact on their son's life when Joey walked into the family room and flicked moisture from his flattop haircut at his sister. Sis laughed, threatening to tell Coach that he showed disrespect to a woman. She was just saying that Coach Mitchell would always be welcome in the Samuels' home, especially if he submitted to her giving him a ping pong lesson in the garage on some family night.

The Takeaway

It took a while for Joey to understand the personal impact and far-reaching influence of that game and that of his trusted Coach.
Thirty years later, Martin tapped the pocket of Joey's Little League glove as he spoke in front of a family Thanksgiving gathering. "I spoke with Coach Mitchell recently, and he and I agreed that we need to be reminded of that Saturday morning tie game 30 years ago."
Joey's father pulled out a small notebook-sized piece of paper from his top pocket that had brief hand-scribbled sentences on it. He tilted his hat back off of his brow to gain more light and read Coach's note.

To Team Red,

What a great game you all played. Remember to always do your best. I believe these three lessons from our first game will help.

- Listen to and heed the voice of a trusted coach.

- Be alert to works prepared in advance for you.
- Team up with those who pursue noble missions.

Best Always,
Coach Mitchell

    The family room was very quiet for a moment. Dad's eyes moistened. Mom proudly glanced at her husband with approval as she walked by, tugging his golf hat firmly onto his head. With a confirming grin and wink toward mom, Sis made it known that she knew much more about the essence of life, Joey, baseball, and coaching than most realized.
    The note was handed over to Joey, who carefully creased and folded it, putting it into his wallet for safekeeping. He would show it to many of his former teammates in the future. Dad quipped, "Now, how about we get your Mom to introduce us to that stuffed turkey in the oven. We could all use some of her special warming from the inside out."
    Joey joined, requesting some of her famous coconut cake for dessert. Sis went with Mom to help in the kitchen. Other grownups and cousins and nieces and nephews shuffled around, looking for ways to help. The smaller ones raced for the

swing that hung from the family tree in the side yard. Joey wished he had saved that red hat like dad had saved his little league glove.

On a Saturday morning two years later, the day before Joey went off to a new career assignment in the northeast, he decided to walk the three-block distance to the Princeton ball field. He wanted a glance at the past. He knew that Coach had spent many years in the Little League minors and continued to teach math at the elementary school until recently. He remained close to the kids in their most formative years instead of moving toward a so-called "higher position." Joey reminisced of the many times that Team Red ran the bases in the spring and summer of 1956 and how they scrambled their way to some victories, and sometimes tripped and stumbled their way to losses, but always with a nobility that was instilled in them by their Coach. Joey thought back fondly of his high school years, when he often observed Coach on and off the field, shopping at Publix, grooming the ball-field, discussing sports with his buddies at Pickerill's, or coaching another Team Red.

Coach was always glad to see his former team members, forever wanting to talk old-time baseball, encouraging them to do their best. Sometimes, Joey thought of throttling back on life and just being part of a lifestyle that allowed him to mow some outfield grass while wearing an old batting helmet that muffled the sound of a sputtering engine and quieted the negative and intrusive voices of the world. He wondered if he would some day be able to change professions and give more of his time to teaching, coaching, and serving. But for now, he would go in a northeasterly direction, not a bad choice, but perhaps not the best one. Yet, all worked out for the good.

It was while visiting his mom and dad, during Christmas vacation in 2001 that Joey learned of Coach's passing. Coach's physical heart must have finally given out but not his Spirit. Those close by said he maintained his firm handshake and that determined look from under a ball cap that was pulled tightly onto his head even as he headed for his eternal home from his hospital bed.

To this day, some who witnessed the game in 1956 or who have been told the full story may still wonder, *"Why would Joey briefly pause and glance back as he was racing down the third baseline, toward his destination? Was it merely a natural reflex action because he was just a kid? Or, was it because Joey placed an extremely high value on his prized covering given to him by Coach.* Perhaps so, along with many other possibilities, but it may have been that Joey desperately longed to hear clearly the distinct voice of encouragement and instruction from his trusted coach as he headed for home.

Coach – "…a person who teaches and trains the members of a sports team and makes decisions about how the team plays during games.
- Merriam-Webster.com

A Sage

For the second consecutive year J.R. found himself standing on the 18th tee of his favorite golf course, on a springtime Sunday afternoon, all square in a match against his chief challenger, Larry. One more hole could decide who would be the club champion. Larry had evened the match at the previous hole with a remarkable chip-in birdie from 30 feet off the green. J.R. proceeded to miss his fifteen-foot putt, which would have halved the hole and kept him at a one up lead. But now, by either one of them winning any future hole, the title would be decided and with it would come the perk of a year's free club membership.

J.R. tugged on his well-worn golf hat with the University of Florida Gator logo on the crest. He pulled it tightly down, wiggling it from side to side to display his determination and to conceal a sweaty forehead of worry. He had dozens of golf hats, but this one was this morning's choice for such an important match, since he once won the regional high school championship with it atop his head. He readied himself for his turn on the tee by slipping a well-worn golf glove onto his left hand, fastening it tightly with a firm pull on its Velcro band. He thought, *High and long sweeping hook over the trees, for the win.*

Winning did not mean everything to J.R., as it did a while back. He credited his new perception of life to a man whom he had met three years ago just off the 18th fairway of this very same hole. He thought for a moment of that very first encounter and of the trusting relationship that was formed. J. R. was confident that he would be humble in victory or gracious in defeat. He was hoping that he would reaffirm his long-ball reputation on his next swing by clearing the tall oaks that were nearly 280 yards off the tee at the 45-degree left turn in the fairway. Would his second attempt at getting his name engraved on the prestigious glass-encased trophy be a charm?

There were a number of local enthusiasts who took positions behind the 18th green when they overheard the tournament director's walkie-talkie blurb that both J.R. and Larry had pulled their drivers from their bags. The closing hole was a 550-yard par five, famous for demanding two herculean efforts to reach the green in two. Or if you wanted to take the conservative route, you could land your long-iron tee shot somewhere short and right of the turn and lay up with your second, leaving a smooth third-shot wedge to the pin. Both had chosen their longest and fiercest weapons. Larry would go first.

Should either of them clip a tree branch at the top, fate would have three options: 1) the ball would drop down inbounds, which could offer a chance at a low punch through the trees, likely ending up close to the green, 2) ricochet left and land out of bounds, requiring a re-tee, meaning the succeeding shot would be number three, again from the 18th tee, or 3) have the ball kick right into the narrow fairway where you would be blocked from the green, requiring a 30-yard tap backward and to the right in order to get far enough away from the trees to have a third shot short iron over the top, still short of the green.

Only a few mortals were capable of driving over the trees at the dogleg—fewer each year, since the oaks continued to stretch higher and higher into the sky. These two combatants had proven many times before that they were at the top of a list of only a few who could reach the fairway beyond the trees with one strike. Last year, Larry succeeded and J.R. did not when he went out of bounds to the left, eventually losing the hole and the match, succumbing to Larry's birdie.

The most interested spectator on this

championship Sunday was the elderly gentleman sitting in a lawn chair pulled up to a round table just off this 18th fairway, near his condo. He was wearing his carefully chosen head covering, a quite rare golf hat, one that had a Redbird logo on the crest—not that of a baseball team, but that of a particular make of golf club. There was a vacant chair at his side, the one that J.R. had filled many times before during their Sunday afternoon conversations over iced lemonade.

This most-interested onlooker's name was John Wells, but was better know as Jack. Due to poor circulation in his legs, he had recently added a four-legged, rubber-tipped walker that was usually within reach. He told J.R. earlier in the week that even if he had been more mobile and able to follow today's match step by step, he would still prefer to sit in his own backyard that had a view of the fairway and a glimpse of the 18th green through the tall trees.

He could not see their shots from the tee but heard both, and they sounded the same, as the metal ping of their drivers smacked the ball and as each projectile clipped a nearby lofty tree limb. They both landed close enough for Jack to be able to hear each plop in the leafy rough. He could see the distinguishing color of the logos on the white spheres; both were Gators. One shot appeared to be just barely inbounds and the other was questionable.

Jack recalled the first time he heard a young man exclaim J.R.'s name from the nearby 18th tee nearly three years ago. His opponent had shouted, "That's unbelievable J.R.! Nobody hits it that high and far!" Never had his opponent seen anyone take the shortcut route over the trees and then stop the ball in the fairway without it rolling into the far rough.

Martin and Elizabeth

Jack first chose to wear his Redbird hat on a Sunday morning early in 1976. He had a renewed purpose for living on a golf course and wearing that hat, where some of the top golfers in the region competed in high stakes money matches. He was following through with his pledge of trying to make J.R.'s acquaintance ever since meeting Martin and Elizabeth Samuels, J.R.'s parents. They were the friendly couple he met that year and visited often who owned and managed a popular fruit and vegetable stand on a highway near Walt Disney World. Although it was two hours south of Jacksonville, it was on a route that Jack frequently drove when he set out to catch a large mouth bass.

From their first encounter, Jack became a fast

friend of Martin and Elizabeth. They had common ground in their love of fishing and the game of golf. They each had caught a number of good-sized, large-mouths while trolling Lake Tohopekaliga from within small boats pushed along by 10-horse Johnson "kickers." The three agreed that the best fishing lure for bass was an artificial purple worm with an iridescent tip and Jack and Martin both disliked electric golf carts, believing they destroyed the aesthetics of the game and diminished the availability of local knowledge from caddies and their subsequent employment opportunities.

    Jack became a regular monthly customer and conversant friend, usually purchasing a week's worth of fresh navel oranges, some seedless tangerines, and assorted vegetables when he stopped by. The evening dusk would often overtake them before the three said their goodbyes and if it happened to be raining, it was difficult to leave, since the kind couple would invite Jack into the comfort of their motorhome that was always parked behind "The Fresh Crop Shoppe."

    Martin boasted with as much humility as possible, "Do not assume, like I once did, that those who are wearing overall jeans while working at small shanty-like buildings on the side of the road are poor." Martin always seemed to have a wad of large bills that were folded in half in the side pocket of his jeans jumper, but few knew that.

During one of their rainy day discussions over a second cup of freshly brewed coffee, Elizabeth asked Jack, "Have you met our son, Joey, who may go by the name of J.R.? He lives in North Florida near Jacksonville Beach and is quite the golfer." Jack replied he had not but promised to keep an eye out for him and hoped to meet him one day, since many good players walked the 18th fairway near his condo. Some would briefly pass through the out of bounds area adjoining his property in search of their ball after an errant pull or slam hook from the tee.

A surge of hope and thankfulness arose in the hearts of the aging couple since they thought, from what they knew of Jack, that he could be a positive influence for their wayward son. Unfortunately, J.R. had made some bad choices recently that were characteristic of most who gained fame and a taste of easy cash at such a young age.

Achieving only an associate degree, J.R. found it difficult to locate the kind of work that he felt he needed to be able to finance his pursuit of a leisurely high life. He only made, week to week, enough to sustain some raucous partying on the weekends. He was well-liked as a salesman at a popular men's clothier near Ponte Vedra Beach, an upscale community with more than its share of golfers and millionaires. Also, a nearby start-up company called Redbird Sports had trained him to custom fit golf clubs using their different flex of shafts, different sized grips and bendable club faces. With his proficiency for low scores and his expertise in swing mechanics and club design, he was the envy of many of his golf buddies. However, no one had seriously approached him with an offer to back him on any tour, even the mini-tours so prevalent in Florida. Perhaps this was because they knew that he lacked resolve in his character and frequented the wrong crowd, even though his game was as good as anyone's in the region. The lowly consequences of his poor lifestyle choices were evident to most, but J.R. did not see the two as related.

    Martin boasted to Jack that ever since J.R. was eight-years-old he had instinctively been able to perform wonders with a golf ball. He could draw it, slice it, or hit it straight. He could hit it high or low or on a line drive. He accomplished all of this on demand by simply envisioning what he wanted the golf ball to do. There was no list of lofty, cerebral deliberations that he had to check off as he stood over his next shot. J.R. was a natural.

    Immediately following his educationally barren college years and failing grades at the University of Florida, J.R. learned to subsist by shrewdly negotiating money matches on golf courses throughout North Florida, usually clearing at least a couple hundred extra dollars cash on any weekend. Along with the easy money came temptations for fanciful things, like fast cars, beautiful but superficial women and surly acquaintances who drew him into hard drinking at local, late-night lounges. He was open game for providing free alcohol for those who saddled up next to him on a barstool and many liked to just hang out and party with him, because he was a fun-loving guy who usually had a pocket full of money and was generous to a fault. J.R. savored his popularity and continued to hide his shifty behavior from those who loved him the most.

Out of Bounds

During his twenties, five overriding and addictive temptations assailed J.R.'s life: golf, money, girls, fast cars, and partying. By 25, with the help of his part-time job and great golf, he was able to afford a nice studio apartment on his own. He often reduced his hours at the men's clothing store to give himself extra time to practice and play golf matches, usually increasing his gambling income. The latter four penchants filled his hours off the course, particularly when golf went well.

J.R. achieved the rare status of playing to a plus handicap without one single official lesson. With his popularity and giftedness came a self-confident swagger as he approached any tee-box or walked down any fairway within a fifty-mile radius. Sometimes he made $500 in one 18-hole match and there were times when he lost, but never more than $200. The winnings slowly accumulated. Before he reached the age of 27, J.R. had enough cash and a small amount of credit to purchase his dream car—a 1967 Corvette convertible with the largest V-8 available, four speed transmission and the external chrome side pipes with tuned exhaust. His high-visibility lifestyle attracted even more trouble.

J.R. was particularly skeptical of anyone who brought God-dialogue his way. Martin had mentioned to Jack to go easy on the religious stuff if and when he met J.R., suspecting that would end any attempt at building an ongoing relationship. The mention of a lifestyle change in order to be loved or accepted by God, or anyone else was abhorrent to J.R., but Jack expressed to Martin and Elizabeth that he had enough life experience and savvy to know how to tread lightly.

J.R. was headed for a big payday one Sunday morning in late March 1976. He was one up in his high stakes match when he launched his drive in the direction of the blue sky above and beyond the tall oaks at the infamous 18th hole near Jack's place. Four seconds later, J.R. heard the disappointing sound of his ball striking the very top of a tall tree with a resounding thud. Wincing, he knew he could be in trouble. The other three in the foursome were hopeful of their chances as they realized that there was a strong possibility that J.R. would be out of bounds. They took the safe route by hitting long irons, each landing in the middle of the fairway short and right of the dogleg.

    Par or even birdie should be no problem for at least one of them, and since J.R. was playing his one ball against their collective best, their chances were favorable on squaring the match, being fortunate to break even instead of losing $100 each. J.R. expected that he would be able to locate his ball inbounds, clear of trouble, and he did not bother to re-tee for a provisional shot. In the dark recesses of his mind he knew the difference between "finding a ball" and "locating a ball." Finding it would mean leaving it as it lay, no matter the consequences. Locating it was a cousin to re-locating it, meaning he could secretly nudge it to a better position. Unfortunately, J.R. planned on covertly doing the latter, but only if it was necessary.

    The foursome moved determinedly down the

fairway together for about 220 yards. Just before reaching the landing area of the other three shots, J.R. slithered to the port side into the shade of the trees. He kicked aside the leaves, where he had calculated his ball might have fallen to the ground. He wasn't aware of two keen eyes that had witnessed the original resting place of his errant ball. J.R. called out to his opponents, "Found it!" One of the three rushed over to see if there was proof; disappointingly, there was J.R.'s Titleist with the Gator logo, sitting nicely on a bare lie, in bounds, with a clear alleyway open to the green.

    J.R. began to deduce how he would keep the shot low in the beginning and then have it climb high and far in order to land on the green just beyond the deep sand trap at the front. He felt that the match had remained in his favor since all he needed was one good shot through the trees and a two putt birdie in order to most likely win.

    As the three others studied their next shots from the fairway, J.R. heard a man-made sound from behind him that came from a metal spoon being stirred through an icy drink. He glanced to the rear and saw an elderly, gray-haired gentleman sitting about 20 yards behind him in a lawn chair that sat next to a round, metal table under the cover of an umbrella. J.R. was quite surprised that this old-timer wore a hat with the distinctive Redbird logo on the crest, an image that he knew so well. He didn't recognize him as ever having come into the golf shop but immediately sensed hope for solidarity.

The man raised his half empty glass toward J.R. and said, "Good day young man." J.R. replied respectfully, "Hello sir. Sorry for the intrusion." Jack offered a friendly, lighthearted response, "No worries mate. I am used to having people drop by. It's always nice to have Sunday morning visitations."

The words Sunday and visitation triggered an emotional concern within J.R. He wondered if this man had seen him relocate his ball to gain an illegal advantage and if he would say anything. From that moment, J.R.'s life took a different course—on and off the golf course.

The other three, being farther away, took their shots first, and each ended up well short of the green yet in good positions. With fierce resolve, J.R. removed his Redbird five iron from his bag and squarely addressed his ball. He thought about what he wanted it to do and ripped it cleanly between two trees, under the limbs of others and over the green-side bunker. The ball checked up nicely on the green within a few feet of the pin.

The elderly witness struggled to his feet and tapped his glass a few times with his metal spoon in acclamation of golf talent. "Incredible shot young man. Maybe you can give me a lesson at the range this afternoon." J.R. responded with a smile and an affirming nod that signaled unofficial agreement as he strapped his bag over his shoulder for his victorious march forward. J.R. felt confident that the best any of his opponents could score would be a birdie but probably only a par. J.R. went on to sink a 15-footer for eagle to win the hole outright and stole $100 from each of them for a hefty $300 payday.

    Within a few minutes, J.R. tucked fifteen twenty-dollar bills quickly into his wallet. He gave a sigh of relief, since he had been down to only forty dollars when he made the bet on the first tee four hours ago. This cash enabled J.R. to buy everyone of his "friends" in the clubhouse a round of noontime cold beers. Nearby, a voluptuous young woman who served up the celebratory beverages smiled and winked at the rich, young, and handsome winner. She formed her right hand pinky and thumb into the likeness of a phone, held it to her ear and silently mouthed two words, "Call me." J.R. succumbed by tipping his Gator hat her way. He spun off his bar stool, gulped down the remains of his second beer and headed for the men's room. It was only slightly past 2 p.m.

    On his way past the dining area, J.R.

glanced through the picture window that overlooked the driving range and caught a glimpse of his Redbird compatriot who was loosening up with some stretches and turns and deep knee bends. Later, when J.R. reached his golf bag outside, he asked one of his buddies about the man. His friend merely said, "That's Jack. Some call him Sage."

Curious and cautious, J.R. strolled toward the driving range with his five iron in hand, thinking he might offer Jack some instruction. Approaching him, J.R. extended his right hand and introduced himself. The man responded kindly with a firm grip and said, "Hey there young man. Good to meet you. My name is Jack. So, I hear that you won your match." J.R. flinched unnoticeably while introducing himself.

It became evident from his first glance at Jack's golf swing that he must have been a "player" in his day. His clubface struck the back of each ball cleanly, moving slightly downward before taking a nice clean divot just beyond the ball. Consistently, nine-iron shot after nine-iron shot landed close to a range flag that was 120 yards out. His backswing was a little short compared to youthful standards, but his release at the bottom of his arc was pure and effortless. There was no sway, only a balanced turn away and an accelerating turn forward, with his weight never being outside his back foot yet shifting to the front after each strike. J.R. measured him up to be well into his sixties, probably still able to score in the high 70s and must have once been a scoring machine who had to be fearfully dealt with.

Later that evening, J.R. and the barmaid met up, had a few stronger drinks together at his place, and concluded the weekend, side by side in bed, without regrets, before groggily awakening to the late Monday morning light. While brushing his teeth hurriedly, J.R. wondered if she would have made herself available if he had lost the match. Quickly turning away from those thoughts, for now anyway, he surmised how great it had been to hit that shot between the trees, to win his match, to pocket some cash, to throw down a few drinks with his pals and to have his way with a pretty girl all because of his golf expertise.

Meetings

From the very first moment they met on the range, the relationship between J.R. and Jack became stronger and stronger. They seemed to be complimentary, feeding off of each other's passion for the sport of golf. J.R. knew that he wanted to be a protégé of this incredibly talented, well-spoken, kind and gracious older man. Often they enjoyed similar topics, drifting in and out of conversations about Gator football and its infamous quarterback era, their favorite Major League baseball teams, and even about the fine art of shooting pool. But it all eventually came back to golf, at least for a while.

Occasionally, J.R. would feel a twitch of conscience as he wondered if Jack had seen him move his ball back in bounds that first Sunday. Would he ever trust this older friend enough to broach the subject? For now, it lingered in the recesses of his mind but seemed to be moving toward the front. Confession was still way too risky for J.R.

He pondered how the afternoon would have gone if he had taken his lumps and gone back to the tee for his third shot on 18, which he knew would have been the right thing to do. He projected that he would not have won the match, nor been able to buy drinks for everyone, nor would he have attracted the barmaid and would have had to work longer hours the next week. It all seemed at the moment like honesty would have brought a multi-lose situation.

Most afternoons after J.R. had finished his half day duties at the men's store, he would go to one of the many driving ranges nearby to pound out a couple large buckets of balls, working his way through every club in his bag. He ended the evening putting on the lit practice green, calculating the variables of length and slope from all four sides. He loved the sound of the ball rattling into the bottom of the empty cup and thought about placing a portable tape recorder nearby so he could capture that essence and listen to his successes from under his pillow as he fell asleep each night.

J.R. did not know that Jack performed a very strange ritual just before he headed out every Sunday morning to his comfortable, shady backyard station in life. He began by taking a contemplative moment, standing in front of his hat rack. This was his way of seeking numinous wisdom. There were at least two dozen hats to choose from, yet he was looking for the one that would bear the most influence. Perhaps he was considering whom he might meet in the next few hours. Making his choice, Jack would pull the ball cap snugly onto his head, stop for a momentary glance in front of the mirror for one final adjustment, and head out through the back porch that led to his seat at the round table under the umbrella. Each time he strode into his backyard, he looked instinctively to the right, remembering the many times that he had been startled by some streaking white missile hitting nearby. He was well-practiced at patching holes in the screen made by these intruders.

Yet Jack still loved residing as close to the

course as possible. He lived dangerously in exchange for the opportunity to walk out late in the afternoon and hit wedge shots to the edge of the woods on the other side of the fairway. He taught himself incredible distance control with his short irons by maintaining the same rhythmic effort for each swing, while choking up on the club a quarter inch at a time for shorter and shorter results. Many balls would have been lost beneath the muddy water of the marsh across the 18th fairway if he erred long, and with his fixed income from Social Security, he could not afford that. Plus, he was not fond of water moccasins. He also lived dangerously close to the golf course because he longed to meet wayward young men and have an opportunity to befriend them.

    A few weeks after their first out-of-bounds encounter, during a late Sunday morning money match, J.R. struck his drive off the 18th tee, low and to the left of his intention. He was undecided if he should tee up a provisional. He did not. As he walked into Jack's domain, he was glad to see the man and even more pleased that his shot had not hurt anyone and ended up safely inbounds. He considered various exit strategies and decided that he should go for the green. J.R. walked over to shake his friend's hand before hitting his next shot and said, "So, we meet again. It must be destiny."

Jack smiled and said, "I think it must be. Now, go on and hit that shot like you know you can." J.R. didn't do as well this time but did end up close enough to the green for a pitch and putt birdie, again winning the hole, although the match had already been conceded to him three holes earlier.

For those sitting on barstools, anticipating J.R.'s arrival, there would be some disappointment this day, for only one drink would be offered. Maybe, J.R. was cutting back in order to meet up with a friend, but there was no Jack at the range today. The barmaid seemed to have found deeper pockets and was signaling for an alternative local golf celebrity to give her a call. J.R. was right in some respects about how it would have been different with the guys, and with her, and with his life if he had done the right thing by not illegally relocating that out-of-bounds ball a few weeks back.

J.R. hung around for a short while and then felt comfortable enough to drive over to Jack's condo. He waited nervously after knocking on the front door. Jack appeared and kindly invited him to come on in and sit in the back yard for a glass of some ice-cold lemonade. Once they were seated he opened the conversation by telling J.R. about his hat ritual. At one point, Jack smiled sheepishly and said he had often prayed for wayward shots so he could meet new people. The word "praying" caused J.R. to have caution. He hoped that he wasn't in for a religious lecture. He already suspected that Jack knew many of his character flaws, some by way of seeing his temper flare after a poor shot.

The roundtable meetings continued, not so much because of J.R.'s slam hooks or pulls off the 18th tee, but because he volitionally knocked on Jack's front door on Sunday afternoons, forsaking his wasteful time for something better. J.R. trusted him and lowered the bar that guarded his past. Jack began each meeting slowly and graciously, with only a select few easy queries. If he sensed an opening he would move on to more probing queries like these; "How do you make major decisions?" "Are your work and career going along as you expected?" "What are the qualities of the woman that you believe will be best for you?"

No one had ever been able to bridge into J.R.'s soul like this man. A new concept of life crept into J. R., causing him to ponder new choices, and these even made sense at times. What began to manifest itself was the renewal of the mind of a wanderer who was kindly and carefully being led to the juncture of questioning himself on what life was about. This had been Jack's intention all along.

J.R. brought more and more concerns about

his future prospects to the table and less and less of his past. He was encouraged by Jack to stay in bounds in his life by walking a more narrow path. In certain instances, he pressed J.R. to push away from the alcohol, find one or two quality friends, bide his time with the ladies, and draw close to a woman who was best for him.

Golf Tips

Serendipitous to Jack's life counsel, there came J.R.'s way of introducing unique perspectives on how to play the game of golf. In the pre-Jack era, J.R. would often tense up over critical choices, believing that the outcome would be key to his worth, or lack of it. He had previously felt that good golf was the key to a great life. Jack seemed to be reversing that viewpoint, espousing that good living was the key to great golf.

Jack taught that over-using the large muscles could take over the fluidity of a good swing, actually inhibiting club-head speed, shortening the distance of a shot, as well as forcing the ball off-line. J.R. was learning to relax and make more quality golf shots on the course, and also make better decisions in life. Likewise, Jack believed that attempting something grand in one's own strength could diminish the outcome. He said,

"There will be laborious up-hills and easygoing down-hills, but straight and narrow is the key. Keeping it in the fairway needs to always be in the front of our mind." When they reeled back from their philosophical lifestyle discussions and talked only about golf, it seemed that the two were aiding each other's game in a synergistic fashion.

    One day, J.R.'s putting technique came to the forefront and with that came Jack's insightful tips. He suggested that J.R. go through his normal routine of assessing the distance and slope and line of the putt; once he stood over the ball, ready to putt it, do not strike it but swing the putter fluidly back to a previously calculated stopping point, and then gently allow it to swing like a pendulum, letting the ball just get in the way. He said that a heavy headed putter was best, augmenting the swing naturally. Longer putts were different and were more intuitive.

    This would take weeks of practice, but J.R. knew that it made sense to let gravity hit the ball, because it is much more constant and dependable than muscles that have a tendency to overpower and initiate the yips, jerky strokes, under pressure. One day, when it all clicked, J.R. experienced fleeting moments when he had no anxious thoughts over critical putts, especially not how hard or which direction he should hit it, for those were already pre-determined in his routine. Only one thought came to mind: *How far do I take the putter head back before I let it swing through the ball?*

    For many days to come, late into the afternoon at the putting green, J.R. practiced what Jack preached and by the third Sunday morning in June, he got into the zone and won a stroke play event with a 65, seven under par, needing only 24 putts. Also, one of Jack's comments that had stuck in J.R.'s mind that helped him become a great putter was when he said this, "J.R., I've seen your smooth stroke at the pool table in the clubhouse. If you will emulate that kind of touch on the green, most of those putts that are less than 10 feet will drop in the hole."

    Another Sunday morning, J.R. was trailing in a high stakes match when he approached the 18th tee. He wanted to renegotiate and go double or nothing on the last hole. He thought of the financial loss but never thought even once about any illegal options he could apply if his drive went awry. The opponents agreed to the new arrangement. The added challenge of having to hit a great drive to have a chance to just tie the match somehow brought on an adrenalin rush; J.R. never hit any ball more pure than this one. It possessed a slight draw from the moment it departed the clubface and ended up in prime position for him to knock it close for a chance at eagle. As he marched past Jack, he smiled and repeatedly pumped his nine-iron horizontally up and down over his head. He learned the lesson that knowing you must perform well under pressure in order to succeed is a good thing. He called out to Jack after he hit his second shot to within six inches, "See you soon this afternoon. Let's barbeque some dogs!"

In spite of Jack's knowledge that J.R. was legendary for being the longest hitter in town, one day he proposed that he practice a few drives at 85 percent capacity, which for him would mean poking it out there about 280 yards on the fly. No joke. He could really "mash it," as J.R.'s dad used to say.

Jack explained, "There is a problem with always trying to hit the drive as far as you can. Most players tend to want to hit it even farther the next time, even though they had hit it just fine a few minutes before. The way to lower scores is to learn to follow a good swing with another good swing— no more, no less. That's right, just hit it the same again and again, unless it is a delicate shot that needs to be finessed. Plus, there is no need to hook it on a dogleg left or fade it on a dogleg right; just line up toward what you have decided is your best landing area. Fairways and greens rule the day. It may seem boring at first but not after you have walked off the 18th green a few times with low scores."

Trust

J.R. noticed how neat and orderly Jack's home was, with lots of family photos, some paintings collected in overseas travels with his wife and a bookshelf that was full of what appeared to be classics, perhaps the source of his wisdom and gentile nature. Jack was usually the first to open up and talk about his life history and the slow process of gaining a footing on what really mattered. Occasionally he would touch on his sorrow of having lost his wife of forty years in an automobile accident, but spoke freely of his gratitude for her love and life. A photo of the two of them taken as they sat on two Adirondack chairs at the seaside was prominently positioned on a bookshelf in Jack's living room.

J.R.'s life was on a better track because of Jack. There was something therapeutic about being close to a man like him whom he could fully trust. There were even days when J.R. enjoyed work at the men's store and just playing the game of golf for the fun of it instead of for the money. His five senses were heightened, and he especially appreciated country drives and walks near the St. John's River with a wonderful woman he had recently met. He breathed in the refreshing fragrances of life. He did not fear being alone with his thoughts nor falling into the temptations he once thought would fulfill him. He began to tone his body by eliminating desserts and breads, taking in some regular workouts at the country club's gym facilities, and reading some classic literature. At his job, J.R. made better use of his time, hoping to be considered for a promotion and be seen by customers as a kind, helpful employee. He no longer carried the weight of having to depend on uncertain income.

As the relationship between J.R. and Jack more fully matured, Jack trusted J.R. with much of his personal history. He told of experiencing the Great Depression as a child, working on the family farm instead of advancing his formal education, fighting hand-to-hand combat in New Guinea during WWII, marrying his high school sweetheart, and working diligently at whatever jobs necessary to provide for his family. Jack excelled as an entrepreneur in various businesses, raised two children who loved and respected him, cherished his wife, stayed involved in various charities and still had time enough to teach himself the game of golf. Last year, he almost shot his age of 75. J.R. was surprised to learn that he was that old.

Jack was always willing to give a helping

hand to the less fortunate, provided that he was given the opportunity to get to know them and speak truth to them. With his life, he championed this: "The noble man makes noble plans and in noble deeds he stands."

The day came when Jack told of just how he had pre-planned to someday become a part of J.R.'s life. He hesitated for a moment before saying, "Soon after meeting your parents I began looking for just the right hat." At first, J.R. felt offended that he was just some sort of project, but this was quickly invalidated as he realized that both Jack and his parents loved him deeply and only wanted the best for him. J.R. understood that even though the tactics for helping him were put together by one old man, it was the appearance of a providential event one Sunday morning when someone yelled out the name of J.R. from the 18th tee that confirmed the plan.

J.R. became able to acknowledge the failures and faults of his past without dwelling on them. He knew he was once a cheat, a liar, a gambler, a slacker, a heavy drinker, and a womanizer. Ouch! But now, he embraced a life of professing and living in a way that said, even to those who still tried to lead him astray, "No more of that for me." Jack was helping him turn the corner, heading for a full U-turn.

The wisdom that Jack passed on was real life at its best and became more and more the norm for J.R. He embraced the truth that there were painful consequences that follow poor choices, which had a sneaky way of leading to further trouble and away from life's best. J.R. was growing so fast that there were only a few more times that he and Jack met at the practice range or green, since life had become more important than golf. They would soon walk nine holes together, the only time they ever did so.

The Pact

There was a four-part pact that they would discuss with each other on this fateful nine-hole walk on a late Sunday afternoon, when dark clouds gathered, holding back threatening rain. This time together would have a profound impact on both of them—more so on the younger than on the elder. This scenario had been developing in Jack's mind ever since they first met. J.R. was ready.

Jack sensed that Martin and Elizabeth would be pleased with this manner of teaching their son, yet he never told them the specifics because a key factor was confidentially. With this kind of trust between just the two of them for the purpose of living life on a higher plain, there would be no preaching, no judging, and no binding ways of the law—just a guarantee of honesty and openness with each other to ask the hard questions and to always answer truthfully. It was this type of well thought out and unique proposal that earmarked Jack as a *sage—"someone venerated for the possession of wisdom, judgment, and experience."

In their one and only match, J.R. was immediately impressed with how well Jack struck the ball off the tenth hole, their first, as his drive bounded down the middle of the fairway about 220 yards out. J.R. throttled back a little with his drive as to not show off. Jack responded glibly as they marched down the fairway side by side, "None of that backing off stuff. You're going to need all you have to one-up me." During the next two hours, J.R.'s golf game—and his life—would be fine-tuned.

Between shots, the men reminisced about times with their parents, their siblings, their heroes and their careers recalling their successes and their failures. But when the moment came to stand over their next swing, it was all business. Each spoke aloud of their pre-shot routine details for the sake of mutual instruction and feedback later. J.R. was grateful that neither aging nor ill health had yet inhibited Jack from playing an outstanding game of golf, particularly on this day. Ironically, for the first time in any match, J.R. was pulling for his opponent.

A carefully thought out, four-part pact would be introduced to J.R. on the 15th tee and would hopefully be sealed just before Jack turned left off the 18th fairway toward his condo. Jack loved walking and had told many, "The day that I have to ride in a cart to play golf will be my last taste of competition on the course. The feel of the course through the soles of your feet every step of the way is what gives you the essence of the game. Without walking out every shot, there is no proper perspective of the distance, the slope, the true wind speed, and its exact direction. Plus, walking alongside an opponent is the only way to know his character and the makeup of his game. I never look back to see how far I have come. I believe it is best to peer forward, which, in golf, is simply visualizing my next landing area."

Taking it literally, Jack did not make any 360-degree turns on the course but only made short sideways glances of not more than 90 degrees away from his target. He believed that anything more than that would have a dizzying affect on him. Before long, J.R. also implemented this concept in golf and in life by looking toward his next goal.

As for shot-making expertise, J.R. had a

difficult shot into the green on hole 14, where his second shot on this par 4 was partially blocked by a tall pine tree. Jack challenged him to a contest in order to see who could score lowest from here on through this hole. They agreed and Jack dropped a ball next to J.R.'s. Youth went first, hitting a sweeping low hook that passed to the right of the tree, turned hard left toward the green, and only touched down briefly before it bounded with its over-spin into a deep trap over the back. Age went second, choosing a humble alternative, pitching out to the left, to the middle of the fairway, to a perfect distance for his Redbird 6-iron. This was the very club that J.R. had custom fitted for him in the golf shop a few weeks back. Jack then "smoothed" it from 150 yards out to within five feet of the pin. J.R. pulled his hat back off his brow, shook his head and said, "Jack, nobody your age hits it that well." He applauded softly with his right hand fingertips patting the palm of his left hand, golfer style.

After analyzing his difficult downhill lie in the trap, J.R. wiggled his shoes deeply into the sand, almost up to the shoelaces and blasted his third shot out. The ball landed past the pin and spun back, coming to rest still 25 feet past the hole, leaving a tough downhiller with a left to right break. He went first, missing his first putt and tapping in for a bogey five. Jack calmly lined up his short putt and swung the putter head through the ball, moving it straight up hill before it rattled into the cup for a par. That left him only one down with four holes to play.

The lesson here was to take your lumps, don't improve your lie but instead, play to your strength after a setback. J.R. was not aware that Jack had been hitting similar length shots for years from the edge of his condo yard toward the swamp across the way.

While walking closely beside each other from the 14th green to the 15th tee, Jack confessed to some of his broad array of misspent youthful foolishness when he said, "Yeah, I have ridden almost every ride at the fair." He referred to his days of strong liquor that weakened him, lust that trapped him, wealth that overtook him, fame that enticed him, and misperceptions of God that fooled him.

Just before they reached the 15th tee, Jack mentioned to J.R. that he was not the way he once was but had become a new man many years back partly because on a rural golf course in eastern Pennsylvania, where he walked the fairways every Monday in the company of a man who introduced modus for change. At that point J.R. flinched slightly, sensing that next would come the dreaded judgment, the stipulation of mandated church attendance, the pledging of money toward a human organization, and dozens of other spiritual priorities. Yet, all Jack said was, "Everyone needs to valiantly pursue truth, and when found, you will know it to be a Person."

Calmed, J.R. was given the opportunity to tee off first on the 15th hole since Jack insisted. He felt a new release, not just the one at the bottom of the swing arc, but one of succinct hope that a better way to live was coming his way. Jack followed with one of the sweetest shots of his entire life, nearly reaching J.R.'s massive strike. As they headed down the fairway, Jack put his hand on the young man's broad shoulders and said, "I backed off to 85 percent on that one." J.R. quickly responded, "Not too bad of a shot for an old guy who gets the advantage of using a pull-cart."

From the 15th to the 18th hole, Jack introduced to J.R. his personalized life-coaching strategy and its four-part pact. He had reviewed this many times in his mind in order to keep it simple.

   - First, each could ask the other any questions they chose relating to their previous week's activities, thoughts, desires, or relationships.
.
   - Second, the answers had to be truthful and had to be received by the other with a full measure of grace.

- Third, no one else would ever know the substance of the sessions, the questions, or the answers.

- And finally, they would be open to discussing whether they thought their choices were aligned with noble living, or not, and why.

Jack knew that reviewing this would help him as well. When he was young, he believed that in a man's latter years there would not be as many temptations as in earlier times. Now, he knew better, that finishing faithfully brings with it more challenges for an older man than he had imagined.

Applied forward, meeting by meeting, question by question, truth by truth, Jack felt assured that they would move forward, together. Only after the pact was practiced for a while, did Jack want to begin introducing the concept of an omniscient God of justice and grace, known only by a certain breed of people—only by those birthed into a relationship by faith—yet available to all. Jack would offer this mysterious concept in small morsels in order to not choke a young man who had had his fill of "religion" a few years back.

As they reached the location of their shots from off the tee at 15, they realized that they both caught a "preacher's bounce" and were in better shape than expected. Jack's eyes glistened. He knew the next four holes would be his divine appointment for pressing in with the pact. They shifted toward enjoying the walk and talk more than the match as they began agreeing to the four conditions.

When they reached the 18th tee, both were thinking alike, considering hooking it or pulling it into the familiar back yard in order to sit for a spell, talking and sharing a cold drink of lemonade. Jack admitted that he was a little tired and asked if this would be a good time for him to head into his condo for a belated siesta. J.R. understood. They shook hands, sealing the pact, and J.R. proceeded by showing off with a stupendous drive over the tall oaks. It was his way of giving Jack some space. The elder smiled then deliberately pull-hooked his drive homeward.

Jack realized that he was not the one who would be with him for much longer and that another friend would need to come along to take his place. Just before J.R. reached the far away landing area of his tee shot, he glanced back through the oak branches in time to see Jack, standing with the aid of his walker he had left leaning against his chair, and saluting J.R. with a tip of his hat. By the time J.R. had hit his second shot to within a few feet of the pin, Jack had disappeared inside, content that the pact had begun, and saddened that his days of competitive golf may be over.

Championship Match

Back to the championship match where Larry and J.R. had both clipped the top of the trees, J.R. hit a provisional, just in case his first ball was out of bounds. Larry did not. Jack watched from his round table in his back yard, searching for a glimpse of bright white in the rough as both men approached. One ball appeared to be just beyond the out of bounds marker, the other just inside. Larry rustled the leaves near his ball, brushing something toward the inbounds while J.R. did not touch the ground but only glanced downward, touching nothing. J.R. accepted the fact that he was a foot out of bounds. He picked up his ball and walked to the right middle of the fairway where his provisional iron-shot had come to rest. He would be hitting four, while Larry would be taking only his second shot.

J.R. sized up his chances of hitting through a gap in the tree branches at the outer edge of the dogleg. He believed that he could hit his driver off the deck, trapping it on the downswing in order to squeeze it through a narrow opening with sufficient momentum to bound between the two traps, onto the green. He had this shot and did not hesitate to set aside the 85 percent rule in order to apply the full force of his might. He thought, *A low screaming draw with heavy top-spin* and that is what the ball did, landing with some hook spin, finding the opening, catching some long grass in front of the green, decelerating just enough to finish only 15 feet short of the pin. J.R. even after taking his stroke and distance penalty, had a chance for par.

    His opponent was amazed. He called out to J.R., "Man. No human can do that! Great shot J.R." He thought of re-locating his ball into an even better lie, but he knew that J.R.'s friend, Jack, was only a few yards behind him. He still had the advantage, barring any ill-fated consequences. If he hit the four-iron, it could stay low, fly beneath the branches, but it might not be high enough to clear the traps in front of the green. If he hit the five-iron, it could be too high and hit the tall branches and may not be long enough to clear the traps.

    Larry went for the five-iron. He lashed at it with a vengeance in order to achieve the distance, and it was as pure as he had ever hit a ball. Just after he swung, he sensed a gust of headwind and it appeared to be knocking the ball down, shortening its flight. He yelled, "Go ball, Go!" Deaf to his plea, it plugged in the top lip of the sand trap in front of the green. Larry would now be hitting three, needing to get it close in order to have a short birdie putt and win the match. He couldn't believe the timing of that headwind. He took two shots to get out of the trap and then two-putted for a bogey 6. J.R. sunk his fifteen-footer for par to win. Walking off the green to the applause of the spectators, J.R. wondered how many times he would have been better off if he had just made the right life choices.

One Sunday afternoon in 1985, J.R.'s dad, phoned him in his New England home to say that Jack had died of a sudden heart attack while sitting in the shade of the tall oaks near his condo. He said he had learned that Jack was reading a book at the time, one that was small and indistinctive so as to not intimidate anyone. It was a simple, pocket-sized, English version of the New Testament, a waterproof edition his wife had given him their last Christmas together.

A few months later, J.R. returned to his favorite golf course in North Florida. Again, on a Sunday morning, he was all-square standing on the 18th tee. This was a just a friendly match with new acquaintances. He had the honors on the tee from a previous birdie and went first. After they all had teed off, the four of them headed down the fairway together toward their results. J.R. slowed to a stop a few yards short of the dogleg without proceeding to his ball that had cleared the tall oaks. He set down his clubs, took off his hat and graciously conceded the match offering three polite and firm handshakes. His friends were surprised since he had hit such an unbelievable drive over the trees and would most likely be in position to win the hole and the match. As he departed to the left, slipping into the shade of the trees near the condos, he stopped, turned back to them and said, 'It was great walking along with you guys. I'll catch up with you in a few minutes at the clubhouse and we'll talk more about Sage. Cokes and sandwiches are on me.

***Sage** - "…someone venerated for the possession of wisdom, judgment, and experience."
Yourdictionary.com

An Advocate

J.R., now known as Joseph, had to limit his golf to the one and only 9-hole golf course in this small western Nevada town. The youthful, impetuous J.R. was behind him. In his five years here, he assumed a substitute teacher's role for students from elementary through high school, learned to be the well-respected assistant manager of the hardware store, grew in his Christian faith in a local startup church, enjoyed dozens of hours of four-wheeling in the the vast desert to the east and coached the high school golf team. He loved his wife and the adventure they were experiencing. Yet, today, he was regretfully closing in on the final stages of his departure. He was out of work and was being advised to move on.

With only two weeks to go before having to leave his home, Joseph was brushing against ancient cobwebs and ducking overhead floor joists in his dingy basement while scouring for any personal remnants that may have been overlooked. He was in charge of packing his family's final belongings into moving boxes that would soon be stacked into their family vehicle for the move further west. It would be an especially painful fortnight, since he loved it here, especially being with the guys for the early-morning breakfasts over steak and eggs, with friends at the numerous weekend rodeos and festive holiday parades on main street, and with those at church who had taught him and his wife true western hospitality and a simple but effectual kind of faith.

The Book

As Joseph turned toward the stairs that led up to the kitchen he glanced into a dark corner and noticed a frayed string dangling from a dusty light bulb in an area he had not searched. One yank illuminated a wooden desk with a small drawer that was left partly open. Upon his inspection, Joseph discovered a small dust-covered paperback. He considered tossing it in the large, black trash bag he was carrying but remembered the time he discovered a literary treasure in the attic of a friend's home years ago. Those writings had changed his ways and revealed to him a better understanding of life. He lifted the small book with the faded cover out of the drawer, blew the dust off, and read the title. *Desert Toughened*. He clicked off the light and retreated up the steps, cautiously toeing his way up the fragile wooden stairs into the sunlit kitchen.

Around 7 a.m. the next morning over his first cup of quickly made instant coffee, Joseph began to read his newly discovered 150-page book. Below the cover title was a faded black and white photo of a scruffy middle-aged outdoorsy-looking man, leaning against the shady side of an enormous desert boulder, with a caption bearing the author's name—Foster Grubbs.

The glue that had held the pages together at the spine for nearly 30 years was yellow and parched, possessing a crumbly texture that required gentle turns if they were to remain in tact. The print was larger than usual and Joseph was only on his second "cup o' joe" by the time he finished reading the first two chapters. He appreciated the classic, homespun storytelling style of Foster's writing. As he began Chapter 3, entitled "Hold Your Ground," Joseph sensed Foster's shift into types of allegory.

The author had moved away from writing on the trials found in a physical desert to those pertaining to emotional, relational, and spiritual challenges that appear when you feel betrayed and alone; times when you are abandoned at the bottom of a dry and lifeless pit, sometimes called a dark night of the soul. He was quick to admit in his book that sometimes he had been brought low by his own ill-doings, and sometimes by the injustices of others. He stated that the most excruciating stretches were those that came at the hands of close friends, or work colleagues, or family whom he thought he could rely upon. Instead, they pulled away from him, even falsely accusing him. He described how these abandonments caused him to become reclusive and despondent. He was also disappointed in himself in that he had actually fallen for the lie that people would suffice as his primary source of life and help.

    Thus, when time allowed, Foster would attempt to suppress his feelings by tempering his gold fever, packing off into the desert wastelands with some camping supplies, his sharp hand pic, a battered tin pan and a sieve, all of which were within, or strapped with bungee cords to his backpack. Since finding a good-sized nugget many years ago, he was easily enticed into remote regions, hoping to unearth a large fragment of weighty gold. His jeans would quickly wear thin at the knees from excavating in rocky dry gulches and the toes of his boots were always scarred from panning on all fours at the banks of small rain washed mountain runoffs. His hat that he wore in the desert was large and floppy preventing his balding head from being burned and the tops of his ears from being sun dried.

On the other hand, Joseph was basically only a rookie of isolation and appreciated the book's timeliness, since he was currently fighting his way through a wilderness of his own. His town departure was near and his associated disgrace weighed heavily on his mind. He wanted to fully defend himself legally, verbally, and even physically, but was advised by his elders to lay low and quietly move on.

It was only a few years prior that Joseph had risen to a position of honored leadership in this small town, where people accepted him, liked the courteousness he brought to the hardware store, valued what he had to say in town meetings and church gatherings, and esteemed his willingness to be ready to help. He was considered a good guy, and life for Joseph appeared to be on an even keel. But now, crippling denunciations had brought a turbulent maelstrom and increasing doubts concerning the quality of his character. He had not anticipated that this was what life could be like when his primary intention all along was to do good for others. He was inching his way toward his final days in town with the burdensome weight of reproaches, rebukes, and censures. This morning's reading at the kitchen table brought him renewed hope.

The Author

That evening, Joseph began his online search for other books by Foster Grubbs, but could not find any. Since the back cover was no longer attached, he had to rely on the brief biography that he discovered at an obscure publisher's website that listed sketchy autobiographical details about Foster Grubbs. Remarkably, the author's mailing address mentioned on this site was a P.O. Box in this very same town. Joseph quickly reached for a notepad and envelope and wrote.

Dear Foster,

I am reading your book and have already learned so much about overcoming trials. I live nearby. Can we meet soon to talk face to face?

Sincerely,
Joseph R. Samuels

Again he looked carefully at the faded cover photo and wondered if this could be the same man he had worked with for the past three years at the hardware store? There was definitely a resemblance. He knew him as Lee, but only from a distance, since this older man usually kept to himself socially, even eating lunch alone in the back corner of the store while reading a book. He was strong for an old guy, proficient at lifting fifty-pound bags on and off trucks for hours on end. Lee only worked part time, mainly during the early morning hours when Joseph was in the office at the front of the store, tallying the sales totals and receipts from the previous day.

    Early the next morning, Joseph drove to the post office in town and asked at the counter if anyone knew where Foster Grubbs lived. He expected a "no" since he had surmised that Foster Grubbs was most likely a pen name. The postal worker countered cautiously.

    "Are you employed by the IRS, or are you with any branch of the State or Federal government, or are you a salesman?"

    "No sir. I just began reading his paperback book entitled "Desert Toughened" and wanted to meet him while I am still living here."

    Joseph pulled out his driver's license to prove that he was a local resident and went on to mention two friends in town, his pastor and his boss. The clerk responded, "Good enough. Just be sure to approach him respectfully and cautiously." He hurriedly penciled a map on a post-it that would help him locate a small ranch at the edge of the desert a few miles north.

By 11 a.m. Joseph approached the western perimeter of the high plains desert where he had been directed. "Could this be Lee's place?" He pulled to the side of a narrow and dusty two-lane dirt road and looked again at the faded cover photo of Foster. It did not offer enough facial clarity to know for sure. Twice he drove slowly by this modest ranch home with a broad front porch. He saw an older man napping beneath a baseball style hat that shaded his eyes from the bright sun. There appeared to be a shotgun resting across his lap.

Joseph's desire to meet the author of "Desert Toughened" and his hope for a new perspective on life led him onward. This mystery man could be the one he needed, someone who could exemplify toughness and at the same time be an *advocate to encourage him to hold his ground during life's tumultuous upheavals.

Joseph recollected better times, like four decades back when he heard those momentous accolades from his Little League coach, after he ran the bases so well and slid into home, and, when, at the age of 28, he encountered a sage at the golf course, and another time when he was given the honor of speaking at a large Christian youth conference in Leesburg, Florida, in 1980.

As he drove by the far corner portion of the barbed wire fence for the third time, he felt a sudden and strong pull of his steering wheel as the right front tire on his Jeep quickly and fully exhaled. He threw his hands heavenward in frustration as he dismounted his Jeep.

Rethinking the situation, he said to himself that there was no need to fret because he knew he possessed an inherited confidence in dealing with setbacks, particularly mechanical ones. He recalled the manner in which his parents had raised and equipped him. He had an extra portion of street sense from his father, a man who had worn many different vocational hats. Also, Joseph had gained loads of self-confidence through his mother's inexorable encouragement. Joseph tugged down on his camo-ball cap and kneeled in the dirt beside the flat tire.

Weighing most on him recently were the foreboding realities of losing friends in town. Plus, he was bothered that he was currently stranded in the middle of nowhere, without food, or water, or cell towers, or cash, and no previous experience with this type of jack. Reaching beneath the hinged back seat he discovered the leverage tools designed for this situation and a makeshift toolbar that fit the lug nuts. Just in case he ended up needing to sit for a while until someone came along, he was glad that he had brought a jug of water and some peanut butter crackers. He sensed that there was far more yet to be learned once he pushed through this temporary setback.

Two weeks prior, false assertions had been hurled toward Joseph from one work colleague, two friends, and even some churchgoers in town. They brought an air of suspicion and the dreadful, "guilty until proven innocent" scenario. His life goal, since he had turned away from foolishness many years ago, was that of building a credible legacy and that seemed to suddenly obliterated by innuendo, ambiguity, and downright lies. As a result, Joseph felt that he needed a shot of "man up" courage from someone like Foster. Or was it Lee? Meanwhile the cumulative rejections were suffocating him, with no means by which to catch a fresh breath of "stand up for yourself." Those from whom he most expected support remained silent, or perhaps they really did not know which side to take—his or that of the small number of indicters. In some ways Joseph understood their dilemma, but mostly he did not.

"Desert Toughened" revealed the many times Foster felt as though he was facedown, toppled by the heat-seared atmosphere, wanting desperately to stand up and build an airtight case against those who had spoken ill of him. He could think of little else but vengeance. He called upon his faith, which he believed should have quenched his retaliatory attitude, but a deep nerve had been struck causing him to want to hurt some people. It was remarkable that he stayed out of jail.

By this stage of Joseph's Christian journey, he had been taught how to react when persecuted—to subdue harmful thoughts, be a kind person, return good for evil, love your enemies, pray for them and turn the other cheek. He knew that all of these were right and true, although he sensed that they could not always be a man's first response under threatening circumstances, particularly in the heat of a battle for your life, livelihood, and reputation. He felt he could handle persecution, which he expected when following Christ, but was unequipped to deal with libel and slander. The term righteous anger came to Joseph's mind.

He synchronized with Foster, who wrote of mankind that was created by God to be soldiers and warriors, protective and unafraid, standing against evil, and not holding punches when they needed to be unleashed. Joseph needed someone to validate that there was more to authentic faith than the soft-handed approach to your enemies. He wanted to hear about fighting back the very way that Foster wrote of regaining some earthly ground a few times.

There was one illustration in Foster's book

where he set the tone for a little considered situation and how Christ might respond as a fighting man. Joseph had never heard this before. It went like this:

"Suppose Jesus came home from his long workday at his stepfather's carpenter shop and walked in on a band of men who had broken into his family's home, had Mary, his mother, pinned to the ground and were ready to physically harm her and later defame her name. At that instant, would Jesus be passive, or kind, or kneel quickly in prayer, or would he straightaway reach for the most lethal weapon he could find, subdue them with force, or even kill them if it meant saving his mother's life?"

From what he knew of Foster's character in the book, Joseph surmised that he was far more willing to take the retaliatory approach, more so than the docile one. Joseph liked that about him, right or wrong, particularly in his present situation where he and his wife's honor were at stake.

Foster also wisely cautioned in his book that you wrongly align with your antagonists if you succumb to blaming them for your inappropriate attitudes of vile and hatefulness. Yet, he believed at crucial moments there needed to be desperate measures taken. Paradoxically, this response to pain and suffering needed be sourced by Christ in you, for life is not to be a mere imitation of love and forgiveness, kindness and valor, and courage and protectiveness; but all of these and more are to be a living participation of Christ who indwells believers.

    Joseph liked that there was a common thread between the two of them, of Foster's foundational approach to living a full life across a wide range of acts prompted by faith, some by taking a fighting stance and some by laying down your life. He wanted to ask Foster, "How can you know in which direction the pendulum is swinging? When is it fight and when is it flight?" Joseph somehow knew that answer would not come from Foster, because wisdom would say, "Find the succinct leading and command of God, His present leading voice." It was at this moment that Joseph pondered the difference between the Commandments, ten in total, and a command, Christ's specific instructions, the hundreds He gives each day.

    Many times in his checkered past, Joseph had foolishly fallen into severe trouble under his own power, misled by his own desires and lusts from his own dark side. He had even boasted at times of being unafraid of any lethal consequences, and often gambled with life at the expense others, betting it all on chance, while tottering on brinks of disaster. Imprudently, he believed that his careless ways would never catch up with him, or take him down. During these episodes Joseph had an "I'm invincible" attitude, succumbing to the "pleasures of sin for a season", throwing discipline aside rather than walking circumspectly. In other instances, he may have just slipped and fallen or been fooled, but would tend to regain his rightful conscience and composure with what later proved unfortunately to be only a small and insufficient measure of worldly sorrow, not the godly kind.

  Joseph knew that even now, although a changed man on a new road, he could not claim faultlessness. Recently, he confessed his anger before some friends, asking for forgiveness, but still, the gradation of lies about him from the past few weeks far outweighed any of his earthly understanding of the principle of reaping and sowing. Selfishly, he had hoped his anger would hold attackers at bay.

  Joseph lamented that those whom he thought would have maintained loyalty, or at least would have better understood because of their own sin, their inherited flaws, who now reside in a state of Christ's forgiveness, were the ones who brought his deepest pain. He was beginning to wonder if he had a bull's eye painted on the back of his hat. The forays came high and hard, sometimes just brushing him back and other times glancing off his temple as he ducked and hit the dirt. Some flattened him with such force that he doubted if he would ever trust man again. When he attempted to defend himself, it only became worse and the suspicions grew.

After completing Foster's book, Joseph knew he could not stand on his own against the growing firestorms. He was sinking fast while trying to hold his ground, digging his fingernails into tiny granules of hope that gave him no forward or upward momentum. He wanted to be isolated from human beings, yet longed for someone to be with.

Not to leave any stone unturned, Foster had written that there were invisible dark forces at work that desire to hinder any man's forward or upward progress by undercutting his proposed acts of humility or silencing his sincere cries for help. Also, there was always the enemy's numinous role of misinforming people with destructive, circumstantial evidence. Untimely incidences had added to be a perfect "sandstorm" that was now trying to engulf and decimate Joseph's life of meaning and purpose.

Meeting at the Ranch

As Joseph began to unbolt his jack in order to replace his flat with the spare, an elderly, slow-gaited man with a waist-high, crooked tree branch used as his walking stick approached him. He eased toward Joseph through the creaky gate of his ranch that he kept securely locked. The unsettled dust in the air caused by a recent passerby made it difficult for Joseph to see his facial expressions to determine if the man was friend or foe. The bulge on his right hip indicated that he was armed, but his casual demeanor indicated that he had no desire to bring harm. Joseph recognized a trademark Lee Jeans baseball hat atop his head. It was Lee!

The rounded brim of this hat did not completely shade his glittering blue eyes. Joseph realized at that moment that it had been two weeks since hardly anyone from town had made eye contact with him, but Lee, even though he knew of the rumors and accusations relating to Joseph, offered a kind smile every time he passed by him at the hardware store. Again, Joseph saw that same smile,

Lee welcomed Joseph by pulling his fingers away from his sidearm pistol and reaching forward with a full handshake. The old man's grip was strong, giving a lift to the man kneeling in the dirt as well as a boost to his low countenance. Before Lee released, he nodded and gave Joseph a closed mouth grin. Joseph blinked. Lee did not. Cowboy boots added height to Lee's short frame, but his bowed knees gave that back. Still, he seemed taller than in the workplace, probably because Joseph had read his book, which in his mind added stature to Lee.

"Hello there, Joseph. Glad to see you. I was hoping we could get together before you left town. I hear you are going through a growing stage."

Lee continued, "I watched you pass by and recognized your white jeep. I love its tuned muffler. Come on up to the house so we can get out of this scorching sun. My wife knows what a cold drink of lemonade can do for a hot and thirsty man. Let me call my friend next door to come and fix that flat for you."

Overtaken by his kindness and dehydrated from the baking sun, but more so from the curtailed friendships, Joseph gladly accepted these offers and followed him to his tin-roofed, easterly facing, front porch. Lee's wife appeared and Joseph courteously tipped his hat in her honor as she glided forward with two glasses of iced lemonade and homemade cookies on a silver handled wooden tray.

They said, one after the other, Joseph first, "Thank you Ma'am" and "Thank you my dear." After gulping down most of the iced drink and taking a bite from the oatmeal cookies, there came some preemptive chitchat, mostly from Lee. He spoke proudly of the polished shotgun that was leaning against the porch rail beside his chair, and also of his ivory handled sidearm. Joseph felt safe from all possible intruders. Lee explained the protective purpose of these two weapons that were at his disposal to ward off, or if necessary, kill coyotes and wolves and other desert varmints; or to warn any intrusive two-legged creatures. He told Joseph that a single blast into the sky would usually suffice, yet he was not afraid to go horizontal if need be.

Lee went on to say that by just reaching for his sidearm or shotgun while stationed on his front porch, he had chased away many invasive-minded strangers. Sometimes a stern glance was all it took. He could usually assess a man's true need for help by his gait, the cast of his eyes, and his posture. Joseph must have passed the test. Yet he learned later that it was also because he had demonstrated a respectful caution for Foster's private domain, while rumbling quietly by in his V-8 powered CJ5, without thoughtlessly stirring the dust on the road that fronted his home and acreage.

Joseph then clarified how he had discovered

Foster Grubb's book in his attic and how much he liked and appreciated its style and message. Joseph said, "I did not know you were a writer." "Not many do," the man joked. "Please call me Lee." And that was that; no more Foster from that point on. Joseph learned that Lee's birth name really was Foster Grubbs, but he wanted to live undercover and be known by just Lee, otherwise someone might discover past indiscretions that could prevent employment or hinder acceptance and trust from others.

    Their first meeting at the ranch was short since Lee had to be at Jeff's Hardware by 2 o'clock to man the post of a coworker who was in the hospital. Lee was like that: ready to help where he could and always willing to wear his trademark "Lee" hat and put a good face on the business. Obviously, the hat was why people in town knew him as Lee.

    Shortly, Lee's neighbor yelled from the road, "The flat's fixed!" Joseph stood readying for departure, tipping his hat toward Lee's wife and thanking both of them. As Joseph neared the front gate, Lee hollered from the front porch, "I'll have a bill ready for you tomorrow for that repair!" Joseph knew he was kidding. It had been a while since Joseph had experienced someone going the extra mile on his behalf.

Desert Jaunts

In spite of his hope for a quick and permanent resolution, Joseph learned from Lee that hellishness could rapidly reappear and even escalate even though properly handled. Lee confessed that barren isolation brought his most painful experiences, since they delayed and sidetracked any noble purposes that lay ahead. One day on a ride into the desert, he professed humbly to Joseph, "In spite of all that the world threw at me, here I am, still alive and kicking, helping another fellow traveler to untangle from the world's ways and move ahead. Life is quite the mystery."

Joseph wanted answers to many questions, one being, "Should I abandon kindness toward others and become tougher, more resilient, and plead for a metamorphosis that thickens my own skin?" In any case, Joseph knew he would be offered help from this man who had been in countless dire straits before. Joseph had been sinking into the bottomless quicksand of despondency but now a sturdy branch of hope had been cast his way.

Lee had learned over the years to believe that faith that deals with changing the outward circumstances and the type that strengthens a man from the inside both have broad measures of hope and truth. Time after time in the old days, Lee had been misguided by temptations, culminating with sin, and then having to vigorously search for a kind of faithful restart that brought resolution and resolve. Before this, early in his life when he had been wronged, all he wanted to do was fight.

Lee introduced to Joseph, two key dynamics of an authentic desert toughened advocate. First, would be the role of protecting against the rudiments of the desert that bring physical death, and second, would be staunchly defending the resulting pain that desert experiences must often bring.

Lee's skin had become leather tough, and he feared no creature's bite, yet his inner being still felt the excruciating sting of another's traumas. He had uncanny insight into the whys and hows of desert trials, yet he often had no choice but to stand back and watch people suffer and become more and more deadened. He knew that without a proper warning received and a valid extrication pursued, very little would be learned.

By their fourth ride together into the desert, through the art of conversations for life and recalling portions of his book, Lee taught Joseph how he believed that there were three primary categories of trials that could render a man helplessly lost in the desert.

First, there are physical trials—those bruises, breaks, and diseases that affect the body. On one side, there are those maladies of the body that are healed by medicine, exercise, and diet as well as by the Lord. On the other side there are the chronic physical trials that are not ever healed and must be courageously accepted as God's sovereign will.

Second, there are the emotional trials that weigh people down, usually beginning with wayward, inappropriate thought patterns. Left unchecked, these contemplations depress and delude people into retreating altogether from life, even though they are physically quite capable of proceeding. They may cause people to lash out with murderous intentions. With a soul oppressed by harmful thoughts, one may passively close down or may attack. This person may find a path toward thinking clearly that allows moving on, or remain dark minded that results in physical, emotional, and spiritual incarceration.

Third, are the relational trials and loads that may be too heavy to carry without the help of another. These helpers come along to demonstrate loyalty with an "I got your back" allegiance. Ultimately, they assist a person who needs a kick in the backside, or a pull forward, or a word that leads toward divine trust and comfort. They know that when all self-helps are depleted, a man's candidacy for higher intervention is increased, and God moves into the humbled man to provide strength and comfort.

Joseph experienced the last two illnesses but not the first, for he was not physically injured or diseased and was still young in relation to having any age-induced ailments. He could even be called too young, at least experientially, since he had overcome or escaped so many of his trials in life far too easily.

Since he had recently become the object of false accusations, Joseph felt deserted like never before, and this time the way out of the desert was not as simple to find. He began to realize that many times before, he had just jumped over or crawled under the bordering fence that separated the tasteless sand from the nourishing pasture. Ultimately, the application of those two escape measures left Joseph unchanged and shallow. He would just sneak out of the desert, crawling beneath the obstacles under the cover of darkness or jump over the fence on a dead run. Lee taught that these conventional flights brought no genuine healing, for they contained no effectual confrontations with real-life problems and with those people who had assaulted. He firmly believed that one key ingredient was needed to be victorious and that was to forgive those people who were bringing harm in the earthly dimensions. Lasting progress would only come through the door of pardon.

Just before one of their many, early morning, bone-jarring rides into the sands east of Lee's ranch, he asked Joseph, "Do you have a dessert theology or a desert theology?" Joseph caught the implied difference and knew where Lee was going. He braced himself, knowing this could be a long, rough ride, and he clung to the overhead roll bar at their first major rut in the sand.

Lee said that sometimes all hell must break loose for a man to be free from the emotional or spiritual maladies that beset him. These often come unexpectedly, overtaking a man, engulfing the body, soul, and human spirit, but not *the* Spirit. Thankfully, though hard to believe at the moment, desert familiarity well equips a man for walking along steep cliffs with dry ravines of despondency on one side and depression on the other, while fear of falling prevents other men from progressing safely along these treacherous routes.

New Perspective

Lee told Joseph that he had listened long

enough to people who said that fighting evil with some measure of your own wrathful flesh and blood was always wrong. He said, "Ineffective, peace-making twaddle is often presented as some type of passive solution to a violent physical, emotional, or spiritual attack from the dark side." Lee knew that Joseph was looking for a secure handrail or an embedded, sturdy rock that holds beyond the temporal solutions offered by many religious theorists. He knew by now that Lee stood for fighting back, when necessary, to valiantly protect or forcefully advance, if not by one's own strength, then through the assistance of an intrepid friend.

Lee spoke directly from his book, "Your gateway into this remote, dry region could have come about because of something that you know you did wrong, or because of something that you didn't know that you did wrong, or because of something someone else thought that you did wrong, or because of something someone else thought you didn't do right.

He joked, "Are you confused yet?" He continued, "These condemning people seem to be extra aggressive when you are making solid progress, bearing the torch of truth as others near you find freedom. Those who rise up to slander and gossip want others to believe that they have the inside dark scoop on you. Pride overtakes them and traps them the very instant they speak against you. From then on, it is a long way back to confessing that they were wrong, for by then, many have enlisted in their army of character assassination. There are some egregious acts that bring irreparable consequences this side of heaven, moving about with the wind, like feathers that are shaken out of a pillow in the town square. There is no way to put them back in their place."

In his experience with such detractors Lee confided, "There is the need for a higher sustenance to rise up within the falsely accused in order for him to survive. You may someday even be thankful for these types of vicious perpetrations. A dark night of the soul may come your way in order to test your metal as one who is destined to be molded and strengthened as a battle-tested soldier. Some say all bad situations are a payback for sin. Nonsense! I believe there are three heretical variations that can be falsely assumed."

Lee explained, "First is the one that blames all discomforts on the devil, with man having no fault. Second, is the one that blames it all on man, with no diabolical power involved, whatsoever. Third, is the one that God could not be a God of love or this suffering would not have happened."

Joseph and Lee interconnected more deeply, believing alike of the varied situations used in the sanctifying role of the Savior. They agreed that any days of testing in the middle of one's own personal desert could have been brought about by some type of justice or injustice, by riches or poverty, by the abandonment of a friend, or by too many friends, by divorce or by marriage, by success or by failure, by greed or by generosity, and on and on, each or all with the consequence of rendering one in desperate need of wisdom and power beyond oneself in order to reach for and take the higher ground.

Perhaps the most confirming portion of Lee's writings and personal counsel was where he proclaimed, based on his own experience, that an antagonist's dark-sided intention was not to be the final chapter of any man's life. He gave many examples of his battles won from what appeared to be a hopeless position in a destitute physical, emotional, and spiritual state. In his explanation of the highest good not being stopped by evil, he summarized the circumstances and ultimate outcome of the biblical Joseph, son of Jacob.

The two men's agreements accumulated as both recognized that the enlightening moment of anyone's unmerited favor may be when there comes the realization that there has appeared an earthly advocate, a defender, a survivor, one who is toughened, who has been prepped to walk with you for a season. Lee had long ago discovered one such person and Joseph now had one. This person will give you the reasons for supporting a "desert" theology rather than a "dessert" theology.

    Lee reminisced of the lasting benefits of his times in the desert and the friends who helped him survive until he found the way out. Joseph was learning that men like Lee were atypical, for in spite of their pain and anguish, they emerged stronger. Such godly men do not believe that the smooth sailings teach very much, nor do their lives consist in the abundance of material possessions. Instead, it is usually in the barren times, the storms, the deserts, the rugged climbs, the failings, in the situations that most men would never choose on their own that cause men to be thankful in all circumstances; then and there they find an inherent strength that is available through faith in an all-sufficient God.

    Joseph gained much from reading the book but a greater amount from listening to Lee as they jolted along, four-wheeling in the wilderness. Joseph was being changed and now believed that no matter how one arrives, high or low, full or empty, in delight or in despair, one must live in the present and listen carefully to the voice that equips, firmly grasping the helping hand, believing in divine intervention, and trusting in a transcendent God of mercy and grace. Lee professed that there was a table in the wilderness, mentioning the spiritual feast that the Lord prepares for us in the presence of our enemies.

Lee said that during the traumatic events in a man's life, there may be only a few who are close enough and alive enough to assist, pray, console, encourage, or kick your rear forward and then be willing to pull away, becoming less and less as God becomes more and more. On the other hand, there can be too many who are close by who want to cling to you when all is going well and run from you when the tide turns. Wisdom says that a friend will not become weary in well doing yet also says that you must sense the pain of being left alone at times or you would not learn strength beyond the natural.

Lee cautioned that it was immediately after the distribution of his book, many years ago, that his assailants turned up the heat, judging him from afar, without the fortitude for face-to-face discussions. And depending on their view of what his wrongs were, or how his bad counsel could lead many astray, they cautioned others against reading his book. Thus, only a few copies had made it into the Christian market, or any other market. Some who had spoken up for him in the beginning were now speechless and had drifted away, not knowing what to say or do. A few had fabricated other lies, denouncing his character. These took no further steps with him at all, as they assumed the worst about him, completely disengaging, considering him to be infectious to any ear that was open to him.

In perspective, Joseph had only been accused of misappropriation of funds that the hardware store was gathering for charitable purposes. Yet, it would take several months after he and his family's departure for this to be proven otherwise, too little and too late for his credibility to be regained in his field of work in this small town. Lee said, "Such is the way God may scatter His own for the good of reaching the whole world."

Six months after leaving town, Joseph seemed to be slipping again into despair, when a gracious couple, sent by friends from the same small start-up church, stepped off a trans-Pacific flight into their lives to reconfirm God's ways and Joseph's worth and work. They, like Lee, offered a sound perception of life that allowed Joseph to press on toward his high calling. Remarkably, because of Joseph's altered course brought about by this small town incident, he and his wife discovered a deeper and truer sense of how to be used for the needs of others in developing countries like Sumatra, and Nepal.

Joseph was glad to have learned that there

are a few tenacious friends in a lifetime, who hold with you on the battlefields of life through all sorts of deadly assaults and a few others who return to your side, foregoing the past. The doorway for these reconciliations is opened through humility and tearful moments of forgiveness on both sides.

    Joseph was brought to the resolution that a trustworthy friend during formidable times will dig a foxhole for two, crawl inside beside you to defend you and teach you life. This advocate stands guard with you, ready to draw a sharp blade, physical or spiritual, and slash it toward all threatening foes. He is the one who listens carefully to your side of the story and yet does not fear getting in your face with personal rebukes, if need be. He is not afraid of fiercely admonishing those who are stirring up trouble in your life, those who resemble the chaos brought on by devil-dusters that sweep across the desert landscapes. This friend locks arms with you and pulls upward, helping to release you from the sinking sands of "Why me?" and the deep valleys of "I cannot go on." This brave soul lives out the vow of "leaving no brother behind," as he strives for your highest good, laying down his life for you.

    Through it all, only someone like this is willingly to endure, without flinching or regret, the fallout of accusatory shrapnel, the personal collateral damage from the verbal grenades lobbed your way. During his tenure with you, he is not frightened when foes encircle your camp with slanderous voices and libelous leaflets, but he proudly identifies with being added to their enemy list on your behalf.

Authenticity

Joseph observed in Lee an authentic life of faith lived beneath the ever-present frayed and dusty head covering of a tough guy. He often witnessed a determined grimace that resided in the shadow of its brim. This fighter had unkempt stubble that pushed its way through a sun-weathered face as he peered at danger through squinted yet clear eyes that seemed to measure the depth of anyone's resolve. He needs to be considered as an ally as quickly as possible, a newly found point man, who calls out battlefield instructions in the midst of the blinding, swirling sand. He does not need to be complimented by you or told that you appreciate his expertise and help, for he doesn't need that type of exoneration to maintain his post. He rightly surmises that you will stay close to him and not run away when he confronts you with your weaknesses and faults. He presses on you to live in the here and now, in the moment, and may be the only dependable, earthly counsel that you will have until you can hear from Wisdom, again, firsthand.

Speaking one day from his shotgun seat, Lee said that city folk often label desert warriors as crusty, unkempt, eccentric, stubborn, vulgar, calloused, and political and religious extremists. Yet these types of allies do not back down from any snakes, scorpions, or demons, for they are able to shoot, stomp, or rebuke them. They wear a righteous right-wing chip on their shoulder, as if it was a badge of honor but know where to draw a line of demarcation that is best suited for maintaining both truth and friendship.

These soldier's hats have no need for chinstraps, for theirs are handpicked and tightly secured against all the swirling overhead elements that intend to harm. The blazing sun cannot scorch their heads in its effort to crisp-fry their well-connected synapses. All of their outer attire is grossly faded into non-descript "desert beige" by the extreme elements and strong laundry soap. Each morning, they pull on their tight fitting, mid-calf boots and look forward to driving out in an ancient yet durable four-wheel vehicle with a cracked windshield that is in its place more for the purpose of blocking the pelleting sandstorm than for the intent of seeing clearly the ruts in the road. They return each evening, weary and needing repair, so they first hug their faithful wives before saddling up to the candlelit dinner table. Vehicular maintenance is accomplished with the help of a neighbor who has bare spots under the shade of nearby trees that he calls his shop.

    This valiant defender has honed his skills of gunnery by shooting through the cold night at any thieving, murderous types, usually needing to use but one of his many well-oiled weapons, the one closest by. Most such men lack credibility at first glance, yet they have a blend of fierce loyalty to God and a purified, on-the-edge sense of the raw retaliation against spiritual and physical enemies. For them, loving their murderous enemies is more akin to putting the fear of God in them by hoisting a loaded pistol in their right hand, rather than approaching them with some kind of far eastern, high altitude guru style mantra, with an attitude of cross-legged pacifism. They will have experienced numerous falls from the narrow ledges, taken a few backward tumbles into deep pits and long directionless wanderings as blinding sand is blown in their faces, yet they are willing to admit that many of their tribulations were self inflicted, not the cause of others.

    A true advocate, like Lee, remains firmly at your side, your front, and your back, proving himself to be an earthy rock of a man, tethered to the truth you need to know, delivering it in small bits as to not choke you with its hard-to-swallow grisly chunks. From ones like him, you will sense a relational binding that you do not want to ever untie or have severed by an other person. He will not accept any self-pitying platitudes from you, and you will learn from him not to hold to the advice of any who only want to enable you to blame God and others for any faithless attitudes.

Joseph knew from the Bible, and from Lee's book, that vengeance is to be from the Lord, and that there is the need for caution in considering this to be man's role. Yet, temporarily positioning yourself in a retaliatory realm is common in the nature of all valiant combatants, even Christians. And it may not be wrong at all for a man to be fierce and forceful, ready to apply the left hook to the jaw of anyone who refuses to back away from attacking a brother or a sister or the defenseless child who is being unmercifully attacked and battered.

Toughness

Lee was puzzled that so many see soldier traits as disqualifiers of true Christian character. His comeback was, "Haven't many of us known all along that life is a physical, emotional, and spiritual fracas, not only brought about by dark invisible forces in heavenly realms but also by the nature of man's carnality. Don't we all need a proven battle-scared friend, an earthly role model with gutsy insight to remind us to "man-up" and use our weapons of warfare appropriately against all attacks? Unfortunately, we have been taught by ritualistic religious leaders to retreat from frontline duty, like pacifists who are fearful of any hand-to-hand combat. We should know that anger can be used to raise our righteous blood pressure for the good of others. We need meaningful, visible acts of war for others to see love on the battlefield in order that they know that the courageous will defend them, laying down their lives for them, for there is no higher love. Like Christ, we can rebuke and display anger toward those who try to disrupt lives and the Kingdom of God."

    Lee continued, "Christ always lived within faith and listened to the one proper and correct voice—His Father's—for personal commands. He was publicly outspoken against and physically offensive toward righteous pretenders and religious thieves. He lived out the personal command from on high as He swept the temple clean of its moneychangers. When He said who He was in the garden, soldiers fell to the ground in the presence of His authority. We can say that He knocked them to the ground, if you will, and was not overly concerned that they might be hurt and bleeding in the fall. When it was time to die, He did so without blaming those around Him or whimpering about the unjust situation or other circumstances."

Joseph finally came to the place of reconsidering his recent passivity toward his false accusers and thought, *Is righteous warrior-hood an anathema to true faith, or should it not more so be a requirement for any soldier of the cross?"* Lee had written, "Is it not good and liberating to know that crossing over the line called retaliation in order to make truth and justice known can be a life-offering act?"

Joseph began to understand that everyone needs close-by friends who are living on the edge, where faith is so often demonstrated by a person who is not afraid of fighting for you, even when he has to risk traversing the border marked by the walls of legalism that are set as a standard by those who believe that law supersedes grace or that fleeing supersedes fighting. True advocates will fearlessly and faithfully charge ahead, in defense of a just cause, proclaiming by their fervent loyalty that it is not sin itself that keeps you, or anyone else, from heaven, but only lack of faith in the One who paid for your sin.

This measure of grace was rare in Joseph's life, and he now believed it widened the battlefield for anyone who fought along the blurry, dusty, indistinguishable front lines of desert warfare. This type of fearlessness within a man is not often found, since most want to run away from the skirmishes for justice, or quickly slip downhill to make themselves known in a safer, demilitarized warzone. Any Jesus follower will fall or even take a knee-jerk leap to the wrong side at times, even to the point of losing temper or sinning in other ways, yet he is still emboldened to take action both offensively and defensively. When anyone puts a toe near that divine line of demarcation between obedience and disobedience, it can be puzzling as to what step to take next. Yet without a willingness and a notion to cross that line, men can become inert, frozen in place by indecision or knocked backward because of their flat-footed stance against the frontal onslaughts.

    Lee said, "Truth is, once you have been through this kind of wilderness and know how harsh it can be, you may be seduced toward retreating into a comfortable, isolated, high rise, city dwelling that towers above real street-level living. Or, hopefully, for the best of others, you will strive to be that rare breed of man, who helps a struggling brother who is sinking fast. Therefore, go and make another of the same species, a disciple, who, too, will always be on the lookout for those who are lifeless and facedown with hungry vultures gathering overhead. If you only occasionally descend from comfortable places to stare blankly at those who are dying in the desert, you are of no help."

Lee cautioned that no one ever wants to taste the grit from the wake of sand that has been pushed into his path by anyone plowing a death row. Yet it is best for the lost and dying if we stay near them, since they are usually too prideful, or too delusional to ask for help. There with them, we learn to listen and to give the answer for the hope we have.

Years Later

Joseph, in future conversations, was able to tell many that if you want to find an advocate—a person who supports others and helps make their voices heard —you might choose to first look for one who is firmly booted in work-grade blue jeans, who has a gun rack on the inside back window of his pickup and a "Jesus Saves" bumper sticker. He will love cruising the desert, and usually he will be beneath his favorite dusty, dirty hat. If he appears gruff and anti-social, it is because he is. But, don't be afraid of him, for he does not cater to men who fear men but is more akin to those who say it like it is regardless of anyone's snake-like venomous recoil.

If you get a chance to ride off into the desert with him remember to hold on, for there will be no seat belts built into his aged vehicle; it is far too old to be outfitted with such manmade legalities. It may be slow going on the drive out and even slower on the return since a couple of gears may not function well and the engine may easily overheat, even on a cool day, because the radiator has swallowed too much grit.

Unlike most men in the world, he will be prepared to boldly open a dialogue about Jesus with anyone—anywhere, anytime. He will have the discernment to follow timely and true leadings and unafraid to ask straight-forward questions, even to strangers. If they respond with shallow, lifeless answers and then only want to be involved in argumentative religious tirades, he will not fall prey to such diversion. Instead, he may choose to shake the dust off his boots and move on.

Oddly, this genre of mankind, the fierce, gospel gunslingers, are those who have the rough exteriors, but actually care deeply from within. They may hold way too tightly to their own bag of selected doctrines, though none will be outside of Christ and who the Bible says He is. Within their new heart, there is no desire to physically or verbally harm others or lash out indiscriminately, but that doesn't mean they won't defend truth and justice any way necessary. They will introduce a just measure of wrath to those who particularly attempt to harm family or friends, should the highest voice say, "Put the fear of God in them." Each will have a forceful dialogue ready to be unleashed that says it like Jesus did, if necessary: "Get back you bunch of snakes and vipers!" They also know full well about the importance of forgiveness, theirs toward others and others' toward them. They look hopefully for any day of reconciliation with those who have sided wrongly against man or God.

    At the end of the day, these valiant soldiers will not crawl under a blanket to stay warm after the sun goes down, but instead be ready to have meaningful discussions by the campfire well into the cold night. They will lean forward into the resistance, march upward into the rugged mountains, or descend into the valleys of death, always with nourishment on board for you first and then for themselves. They will say to you, "Live the Christ-life fearlessly and faithfully."

Grace

    Lee expressed God's grace to Joseph in this

manner during one of their final meetings on the front porch of the ranch. "I'm not sure why I like living here on the edge of nowhere, but from this front porch, at my age, I believe I can almost see heaven across those high sand dunes to the east beyond the cool mountains. I tend to rarely remove my hat except for church, for the national anthem, for the honoring of a friend who has passed, for a lady or elderly person, or for the veterans. But when the day comes that I enter glory, and that will surely happen by way of God's grace, I believe this dusty head covering will be blown off by God's mighty wind the very instant before I am able to reach up and honorably uncover in His presence. And that will be just fine by me, for in that moment, I will know His grace as being more than I ever imagined."

    Upon his final departure, once outside the front gate of Lee's ranch, Joseph resolutely tugged his hat tightly onto his head, looked back at Lee and honorably touched the brim as a salute. He mounted up into his fully packed vehicle and drove off to the west to join his family who had found a safe place. He was confident that he was better equipped to face life's trials than ever before. He was even thankful for his desert era and understood that it came along for his good. Joseph was especially grateful for Lee, his advocate and friend. He would never see him again but never would Lee be absent from his heart nor would "Desert Toughened" and his Bible ever be far from his reach. Joseph acknowledged that his favorite chapter of the book, was the fourth, entitled, "Knowing A Tough Guy", for one such man he knew well.

***Advocate** – "…a person who supports others and helps make their voices heard, or ideally for them to speak up for themselves." - Yourdictionary.com

A Mentor

Joe Samuels had migrated from the West three years earlier with his wife and teenage son. His previous hardware store experience quickly opened the door for some promising job interviews and within the first week the owner of the newly expanded Ace Hardware, Richard, offered him a position. He would be an assistant to the manager and assume some bookkeeping and marketing duties, thanks to a respectable recommendation from his previous employer. His wife, Ann, with her many stellar accomplishments in the field of teaching, had little problem finding work. It was a welcome fresh start for both of them. Their son had loved the west but looked forward to the chance to snowboard.

Joe volunteered to be an assistant to the high school golf coach, which turned into the head position by the time the season began. A few churches were visited but Joe was reluctant of becoming too deeply involved since he was in the process of re-evaluating his own base of faith, which he was currently doing informally with a couple of his friends over coffee and Saturday morning breakfast at a local diner. Joe would always bring a Bible, a pen and a small notebook. He was looking for a way to live out his Christian faith by loving his neighbors without all the bells and whistles of religious formality often associated with organized church functions.

    This particular Saturday morning Joe and his closest friend, Mitch, were discussing how Christianity was simply a "believe in Christ and love your neighbor movement" at its very base. Glancing over the top of his steaming coffee, Joe saw a newcomer, an elderly man in a pristine black leather ball cap, walk into the Village Eatery, the home base for early morning breakfasts for many men in town. The diner was located across the street from the Congregational Church, near the main square in this small New England town. Joe heard this man say to the waitress that his name was William.

    His stature, demeanor, and casual attire instantly reminded him of his desert friend, Foster, from whom he had learned so much in the last two weeks of his stay in Nevada. That was three years ago, but the lessons learned were as fresh in Joe's senses as the aroma of the hot and hardy breakfast sitting before him. Mitch and Joe paused for a moment, giving quiet thanks before digging in. Before the weekend was over, Joe and Mitch would know William even better and be better for it.

It had been a leisurely four-day journey for William Harris, cruising along with his windows cranked open in his small pickup, taking the less-traveled roads from St. Augustine, Florida, up the east coast on A1A. Turning inland north off of I-95 near Boston, he arrived late on a Friday afternoon at the edge of this quaint New Hampshire town. It was more of a village than a town, with no gas stations open after 8 p.m., only one Dunkin Donuts and no hotels whatsoever.

That first evening, William slept stretched across the front bench seat with a pillow propped against the passenger side arm rest. The weather was accommodating enough for him to be able to stay warm even with the windows cracked open slightly. He drifted in and out of consciousness surrounded by the soothing sounds of flowing water nearby that trickled downstream beginning to fill its banks with the spring melt. The sound of birds singing, and the light of dawn breaking through the trees awakened him early. He stepped outside for a few stretches and deep knee bends in order to get his 70 year-old bones loosened enough to walk for a while. Soon, hunger began to slow and, eventually, stop him short of his usual 45-minute jaunt. It was time to locate the diner he had been told about by a native New Englander at his last fuel stop the night before.

William had been on the move for the past five years, evenly segmented into six-month intervals of spring and summer in the North, and fall and winter in the South. It had been six years since his wife, the great love of his life, had passed away. With his children grown and settled with their careers and families, he had the freedom to live and work in small towns long enough to accomplish similar and related goals in six month intervals. Christmas time was usually when he broke stride in order to catch up with family for a week or two of home-cooked meals, photo sharing, storytelling, life updates, and hugs all around.

As he stood by his truck, he envisioned how his next six months might play out, hopefully, similar to the past when he met many friendly locals, hired himself out for some odd jobs to supplement his Social Security income, and culminated his sojourn dramatically with a farewell breakfast on the last Saturday of his six-month stay.

William had learned to live an independent life, much different than when his wife was with him. He took up odd jobs on the road and pursued a meaningful existence by developing a few close relationships in each new community, usually by eating regularly at his favorite diner. He wanted to continue his stroll along the lower banks of the river and step across the mid-stream rocks into the early morning mist, but instead, he slipped behind the wheel, pulled his distinctive black leather ball cap snugly onto his head, fired up his V6, and drove into the heart of a new assignment.

The Diner

After crossing the narrow two-lane bridge into town, William spotted the Village Eatery on the right and sensed it was the place he had been told of and hoped it would be where he could find the kind of clientele and breakfast he enjoyed. He parallel parked in front and seamlessly stepped out of his imaginations into the real world. He firmly pulled open the glass front door of the diner that faced the sidewalk and walked into a gathering of Saturday morning regulars.

Observing a majority of men, he thought to himself that it was great to see so many hats sitting atop heads, even while the guys were eating. He had learned that a ball cap on a Saturday morning in a small town diner was akin to a man's personal trademark when he was allowed to be himself, eat what he liked, converse with friends, and not feel compelled to remove his covering while dining. Contrarily, on the five preceding weekdays, men often feel they have to identify with their job, stay within their diet, and wear whatever uniform the boss requires. On those days their outfits could be anything from a white shirt and tie, with polyester slacks and shiny shoes, to an old pair of blue jeans, a faded T-shirt, scruffy boots and a ball cap with a favored logo. That leaves Sunday; and a man's attire on that day depends largely on whether he goes to church or not. If not, he may wear his Saturday casuals two days in a row, or, if he was a church-goer, he would upscale as necessary but surely not wear a ball cap—at least not into the diner and for sure not in church.

    Being the outsider, William wanted to connect quickly, so he opened a dialogue with the lady cashier about how glad he was to be in this cooler climate and how he looked forward to settling in for a while. He introduced himself to her loudly enough for some diners nearby to hear him say, "Hello ma'am, my name is William." She replied, "Welcome stranger. Good to have you."

    By way of his appearance, he seemed to be, to those who were scrutinizing him, a laborer or a handyman, perhaps a painter, due to his strong looking hands and the multi-colored drippings on his work boots. What was most distinguishable to the waitress was William's quality, well-fitted black leather ball cap. From a table across the way, Joe and his friend, Mitch, had noticed the distinctive looking head cover as well.

The four men conversing at the table that was set perpendicular against the front window, the regulars for early Saturday morning breakfasts, noticed that William drove up in an older model F-150 Ford short bed, with a tool chest securely locked and resting beneath and behind the rear slide window. Also, there were two aluminum ladders in the bed along with some landscaping equipment that peeked through a green tarp held in place by bungee chords. A baking sun had apparently dulled the once shiny red finish of his vehicle. The out-of-state tags indicated the he was from Florida—the Sunshine State.

The other waitress headed his way and quickly sized him up. She thought him to be in his 60s, about 6 feet tall, with distinguished long gray hair; he wore no wedding ring, neither was there a tan line where one could have recently been. His warm smile and friendly demeanor outshone his faded blue jeans, his well-worn red-plaid work shirt, and his loosely laced, scruffy work boots.

William settled onto a swivel stool at the far end of the counter and searched through the menu. He did not bother looking at the right column of the menu, because price was no object when you were as hungry as he was. As the serving waitress reached him, she greeted with a smile and poured steaming black coffee into a large mug without asking what he would like to drink. She knew inherently that men dressed like William wanted their coffee first before they had to make a major decision about their Saturday morning fuel. William saw his favorite breakfast at the bottom of the menu and ordered the "He-man" steak with three eggs, cooked one-sided over easy, toast and hash browns. Once the waitress passed the order through the kitchen window opening, his stomach rumbled, seemingly glad to hear the aproned cook call out "One He-man" coming right up!"

 William paused for a brief moment of thankfulness before breathing in the aroma of fresh brewed coffee that began to bring him to full consciousness. He swiveled 180 degrees on his stool and spoke politely toward the four men at the front table by the window, "Ya know, I love having a steak and egg breakfast where the coffee keeps flowing."

 They were somewhat taken back by his forthrightness but each nodded and the waitress interjected, "Ya got that right," assuring William that he would not have to ask for a refill. The man at the head of the table wore an Ace Hardware hat and it turned out that he was Joe's boss, Richard. He looked his way and smiled, probably hoping to soon draw new business his way. Little did anyone know that William would return every Saturday morning at precisely 7:30 for the next six months.

    Weeks before he arrived, William prepared himself for inhabiting this region by becoming well informed about the local and state politics, its sports teams, employment want ads, apartment rentals, maps of winding country roads that he hoped to cruise, and its churches. Time would tell that it was only on Saturdays that William wore his distinctive black leather ball cap. The rest of the week he wore whatever hat was needed for the occasion, but he was never seen in formal attire. Some would learn to like him and a few would not; others would remain cautious and curious from a distance, as is the typical New England way.

    As he stood to leave, he pulled three one-dollar bills from his cross-shaped silver money clip that was a treasure of his, reminding him of the one to whom his money really belonged. He discretely slid the bills under the corner of his plate. His tab for breakfast was only seven dollars, and those who saw his tip of folded bills may have considered him to be rich, or maybe he was just flirting with the waitress, or even that his math was bad. None of these were the case.

While waiting at the counter for his change from a twenty-dollar bill, he nodded toward some who made eye contact, including Joe and Mitch who were sitting as a twosome at a nearby table in an adjoining dining room. He graciously spoke to the waitress saying, "Thanks. That was a fine breakfast. Kudos to the chef." She smiled and responded, "That hard working man in the kitchen is my husband, and the owner, Ritchie, and we look forward to having you stop by often. Coffee refills are always on the house."

As he took a few short steps toward the front, an older couple was approaching from off the sidewalk and he assisted them by pulling open the glass door that tended to stick at its base because the threshold had been warped by the winter freeze. They were able to more easily pass through and smiled at him in appreciation. William said, "Good morning" and politely touched the brim of his hat. He sauntered down the sidewalk to his truck, eased behind the wheel and turned the key to ignite the well-worn engine. He grimaced when he heard the groan of a weak battery as it labored a few seconds before there was a clunky roar, then all was well, indicated by a puff of smoke that billowed out the tail pipe through what remained of the faulty muffler. He thought about offering his services to fix that front door at the diner, so he could afford some overdue repairs on his vehicle.

    In his first two hours in town, a few people were given the opportunity to see that William was a kind, generous, and respectful man, believing he probably was not rich, was a single, semi-retired, out-of-state, handyman, who probably would be looking for work and some tools. William's plan was in full motion—that of staying for only six months while getting to know as many townspeople as possible, to work hard, to offer himself respectfully and to help the needy, then to move on, like he had repeatedly done before. He felt confident that his first Saturday breakfast at the diner had gone well.

    William drove for a short distance up the winding blacktop north of town to a dirt turnoff on the left that opened into a field and then narrowed into a woodsy walking trail. He breathed in the fragrance of the blossoming springtime as he stepped onto the footpath that weaved its way through the forest. He did his best thinking while walking alone, under his prized black hat that his wife had given him their last Christmas together. He was resigned to the fact that at his age he needed this kind of regular exercise for his muscles and bones and the accompanying fresh air for his lungs.

He began to think about what he would need in order to settle into the village. Renting a small place close to the diner and finding a few pieces of used furniture and some pots and pans would be at the top of his list. He remembered the "For Rent" sign he had seen in the front window of an apartment that was between the big white church and the town's municipal building. He had also seen a couple of "Garage Sale" notices in front of homes that had treasures strewn across their yards. He thought of how much he would soon enjoy taking his first stroll through the aisles of the local hardware store in search of tools and business connections.

He had lived briefly in many towns like this and each time he carried out his prescribed plan but this time he hoped for a little more wisdom and precision than before. He knew he needed to be helpful and patient toward his neighbors, allowing them time to observe him closely in order to assess his character. Someone once told him that it takes a while to make a friend in New England, but once you have one, he is a friend for life.

The Accident

William was refreshed by his hour of walking as clear thinking, exercise and inspiration were needed more than ever by William in order to not lose too much ground to the aging process. There was a spring in his step as he headed back to his truck.

    In the distance he heard sirens and could see flashing blue lights flickering through the tree limbs up the hill. Suddenly, all became eerily silent. He had taken some EMS training so he thought of helping out if needed as he walked quickly up the side of the two lane blacktop. He saw two box-shaped ambulances stopped in the middle of the road and a few people standing beside their cars as others solemnly gathered. Police had already come to the scene to close the traffic in both directions. He thought, *This is a bad one.*

        About an hour earlier, William had driven this same stretch of highway that took a sharp turn to the left just past an old three-story farmhouse. He detected at the time that the right shoulder of the blacktop at the turn dropped off suddenly into some soft sand in front of a patch of small trees. As he drew closer, he could see a rather large man lying motionless on his back in the middle of the road near his crumpled Harley Davidson motorcycle. Emergency medical workers already were on the scene, and one paramedic was performing those sickening motions of pushing rhythmically on a lifeless chest. Muffled crying and whispering emanated from bystanders. A smaller group had surrounded another fallen rider who apparently had catapulted into the bushes to the right, stopping just short of the trees.

William remembered how many times he had leaned hard around similar turns on his high horsepower bikes back in the day. He relished the memories of when he rode some zigzagging asphalt roads on a full dress, Harley Davidson that a friend had given him to enjoy. William had been riding anything, from Lambrettas to Triumph Bonnevilles to Yamahas to Harleys since he was a young man. It was the heavy Harley that most tended to drift outward on the sharp turns. Actually, a friend had sold the Harley to him for one dollar, provided that when he was finished with it, he could buy it back, for the same dollar. It was a great ride while it lasted but the fear of jittery deer bolting across the highway and the appearance of invisible black ice hurried the contract's end.

While standing near the tragic accident, William saw Joe whom he had seen earlier that morning at the diner. He noticed that Joe was comforting a woman who must have witnessed the horror of a man and his motorcycle summersaulting as one, onto the firmly packed asphalt road. Joe held the leash of her small dog as she wept. The biker had drifted to the right and hit the sand on the right shoulder of the road. Apparently, he then tried to recover by turning the handlebars away from the woods. He clung to his bike as it toppled over and over. The woman with Joe had learned from one of the bystanders that she had most likely witnessed a death.

Another rider, the third in line in a string of many, avoided disaster by steering straight ahead, toward a patch of low bushes and small trunked trees. He flew into them but was sitting up, obviously dazed, and was being consoled by fellow riders who had circumvented the accident by braking safely on the road. It seemed to take the bewildered biker a while to comprehend what had happened just in front of him. His face was buried in his hands and he was sobbing.

Helpful words being difficult to come by at times like these, William was gathering his thoughts since someone might come his way for solace. There was no time for anyone in an official religious capacity to appear, and William had been used informally in situations like this before. Three men with helmets in hand approached Joe who was still standing with the woman. William eased their way. Joe led them into bowing their heads and listening to his words of prayer and comfort.

Before most had dispersed, there was talk of reassembling at the roadside for a memorial service, since it was obvious that the one rider had died. William and Joe overheard some agree to a sundown gathering that evening, and one rider said he would make a small white cross in his carpenter shop to put in place on the roadside. Joe and William bonded in this tragedy and agreed, on the spot, that they would both be present.

Just before sunset, William and Joe met together again, hats in hand, at the roadside. There were dozens of neighbors who gathered, and many bikers were respectfully approaching, dismounting, and walking solemnly toward the cross. Joe had phoned a friend at the police station, asking that two patrol cars be stationed up and down the road to control traffic as a safety precaution. Many stood silently near the small white cross that had been hammered into the ground a few minutes before. This time, it was William who stepped forward and asked permission to pray. No one resisted. His carefully selected words brought a measure of truth and grace and hope. Joe knew at that moment that William was a man he wanted to know.

Settling In

That evening, William was able to secure the apartment he had seen for rent. The landlord liked him, shaking his hand in agreement, validated by a cash deposit. William was given the key and began his first official Saturday night in town, unloading his few things into his one bedroom apartment and securing his tools with a tightly fit tarp stretched over the bed of his truck.

    Late that evening, William had dinner sitting at an outside table of the pizzeria near his apartment. He met the young couple, the owners, a husband and wife team, who had saved for years to make this happen. The pepperoni pizza with double cheese was as good as William had ever eaten and he told them so. At that moment he decided to use their take-out services in the future for his Wednesday evening men's meetings at his apartment. By midnight, William was spent; but before he dozed off, he diligently set his alarm for 6 a.m. so he could be at the Village Eatery by 7:30.

    For his first Sunday morning breakfast in town, William cut back to just the basics: two eggs, toast and coffee and wore no black hat, just one of his usual, day-to-day selections. After an hour of talking with patrons and staff over breakfast and coffee, William settled his bill and made his way across the street. This was his first visit to the big white church. He eased into the 8:45 first service and sat quietly in the back row near the aisle. As he had expected, the congregation seemed very kind, the message was well-spoken and helpful, and after the sermon, Pastor Chuck hurried to the back row to greet him, as he would any visitor. After a brief conversation **(the other was too wordy and unnecessary)**, William politely excused himself saying he needed to visit some garage sales, looking for anything that could help him settle in for a while.

Being in church on Sunday mornings became a routine for William, but it would be rare that he would go to the same church twice in the same month. His plan was to be among a wide variety of professing Christians and learn their ways, not to join an organization but only to participate in worship and hear what was being said for his good and for the good of the community. He always carried a small hardbound black notebook with him, as well as a diminutive New Testament Bible.

Departing on foot, William ventured two blocks away to check out some garage sale items that were spread out on the front porch of an older home on Main Street. The two young girls, who kindly greeted him, stood responsibly behind their card table which was laden with their personally handcrafted items. Mitch, their dad, a gracious, well-spoken young man, along with his courteous wife, welcomed him. Mitch remembered seeing him the previous morning at the Village Eatery when William and Joe were having breakfast. Mitch and his wife were very hospitable and asked him to sit for a while and have a cool drink of lemonade on their newly remodeled front porch. To top if off, they offered some delicious egg-salad sandwiches. It was a very pleasant hour and a common ground of faith was discovered and graciously discussed.

    Before moving on to his pickup parked in front of his apartment, William gulped down two large cups of cold lemonade that he purchased from the girls' cold drink stand. He also acquired two of their refrigerator magnets. William knew not to haggle with anyone about garage sale prices, so he rounded up the cost of the two lemonades from fifty cents to one dollar and gave them an extra amount for the two magnets. He knew from personal experience how demeaning it was to disrespectfully haggle over the price for items that could represent a family's hard work and fond memories.

    There was one significant item, a wooden, three-legged coat rack that could hold twelve hats, which he found at his second stop, the farmhouse up the hill that was adjacent to where the accident had occurred. William had just about half that many with him but was always looking for others. He was pleased to discover, along with the rack, a slightly worn Boston Red Sox ball cap. The couple that lived there wanted to throw it in for free, since William had already selected some dishes and kitchen utensils, but William insisted on paying its full price. He heard from those milling around in the front yard that this couple was moving overseas, and everything had to go, except for a few special items that they would keep in a storage unit upstate. Shopping further, William gathered five large coffee mugs. He wished them well as he began to settle his bill that was now all of thirty-five dollars. He insisted on giving them fifty dollars as a way of bidding them a fond farewell on their venture into Arabia.

    Walking toward his truck, William saw a motorcycle leaning on its stand across the road and a man in a leather jacket, boots, and blue jeans standing near the newly planted cross. He had his helmet in hand and was wearing a biker scarf on his head similar to the one other riders the previous evening had worn. He walked respectfully with his hat in hand toward the tall, bearded man with arms adorned with ink and offered his condolences. The distraught man looked up, teary-eyed, and said, "Thanks for coming over." William learned that his name was Chris, and he was a very close friend of the deceased and his family. He was the lead rider from the morning before. After listening for a while, William sensed Chris' anger at God for allowing this to happen. William wanted to but did not offer prayer. He spoke his condolences and mentioned how he was a regular at the Village Eatery most mornings at 7:30, and invited the grieving man to join him—his treat.

On Wednesday afternoon, after some much needed income from mulching Mitch's side yard, William connected with a burly, full-bearded man in his forties who was seated on a bench at the park across from the library. By his side was a purebred Labrador, his well-trained seeing-eye dog. The man's name was Simon, and William had seen him once before, walking with his dog near his apartment on Tuesday afternoon. It turns out that Simon was his ground floor neighbor in the two-story apartment complex. William and Simon mostly shared their common passion and memories of having the wind in their faces while cruising the winding blacktops of America. Simon had once been able to see well enough to commandeer a bike much like those that William loved to ride.

As they were getting to know each other further, a somber line of bikers passed slowly through town. They seemed to be heading to that new cross where one of their compatriots had died. One rider stopped, dismounted and walked Simon's way. It was Chris. As he removed his helmet, Chris greeted his long-time friend, touching him on the shoulder then grasping his hand. Simon thought that it might be him from the distinctive sound of his motorcycle, but had to wait to hear his voice to be sure. Still shaken from the accident that had taken the life of his best friend, Chris remembered William and greeted him with a firm handshake and invited both of them to attend the funeral on Friday morning. Simon responded, "I'll be there." William followed suit, saying he would be glad to have Simon ride with him.

On Friday morning, Simon and his seeing-eye dog rode along with William to the Catholic funeral service in the metropolis to the east. It was a sad event, and words spoken and rituals performed in the building indicated a general lack of clarity as to the certainty of the deceased man's eternal home. On the drive back, William and Simon discussed their views on the requirement for entry into heaven, as they believed it to be. There was succinct and mutual common ground discovered and an oath of friendship began that day.

Table In The Back

By his second Saturday morning breakfast, a few more patrons recognized William, offering a smile or a nod. He had already used his ladder and other tools of his trade toward completing three small jobs that brought one-third of his monthly rent. It had been a good week. The two waitresses glanced up from their conversation as he headed for his stool at the counter, wearing his familiar smile and his Saturday hat, the black leather one. He had eaten at the Village Eatery several times this week but wore a different hat each day. His server immediately placed a steaming hot cup of coffee on the counter along with a warm plate, silverware, two napkins and a glass of ice water. This was the morning that William took another step toward fulfilling his plan. He asked to sit at the table in the back corner, away from the busyness. She graciously obliged and added, "Are you expecting company?" William responded, "I sure am, ma'am, I sure am."

    William ordered his Saturday special, "The He-man". She glanced toward Ritchie, the owner/cook, and before she could make the order, Ritchie called out, "Coming right up, one "He-man" it is." William was grateful that more and more people in town were recognizing him and becoming familiar with his routine. His plaid shirt was the same one as last Saturday, but his blue jeans were new, and his ankle high work boots had what appeared to be fresh grass stains on the toes.

    Joe was sitting at a table by himself this morning, wishing he had someone to talk with and he came over to greet William, thanking him for his business at the hardware store and his words of prayer at the roadside memorial. Joe had also seen William earlier that week, shopping for a file to sharpen his mower blade and noticed he had some used furniture in the bed of his truck. Joe wondered why he needed five chairs for such a small apartment. He felt comfortable while standing briefly at William's back table and asked if he might have breakfast with him next Saturday at 7:30. William gladly agreed, "That would be great. Let's do it." He sensed that Joe would be a key player in his overall purpose for being in town. Joe felt that William would be a good new friend.

      As the waitress returned with William's order, she opened up by asking, "What's with that fine looking black leather hat? You seem to wear it only on Saturdays." This was the first query on that matter and William responded, "Yep, it's my treasure. I wear it only on Saturdays, because I know that I won't be slinging paint or pushing a mower on this day. My wife always told me to shut down work, wear this hat, and go meet with friends on Saturdays for breakfast." And that was how he answered all who asked.

      The next Saturday morning William felt comfortable offering handshakes to the "four town elders at the window," as he called them. They were receptive to him—maybe because they noticed his Boston Red Sox hat that he sometimes wore in town on weekdays. Richard, the hardware store owner was especially friendly and thanked him for purchasing paint and brushes at his establishment. William reciprocated by thanking him for the free painter's caps and some inexpensive, empty five-gallon paint buckets for carrying his tools. William hoped they would invite him to join them someday, and later on they did.

Shortly, Joe joined William for Saturday breakfast for the first time. It did not take long for them to recognize the synergy of their friendship that would be used for the benefit of both. Joe now had a sounding board for faith discussions and William had a key individual who would soon help draw three other of his friends to the table.

Each succeeding week William became increasingly liked, not just for his early morning friendly breakfast discussions but also for his quality workmanship as a handyman, a painter, a carpenter and a lawn care specialist. Some appreciated him enough to invite him to come by and have dinner with them, but he usually graciously declined, knowing that too much familiarity could spoil things. Yet, he did eat a full dinner with Mitch and his family twice and also once with Simon and twice with Joe and his family.

Pastor Chuck bid him again and again to come by for Sunday morning services. William really liked Chuck and his messages, but continued to hold to his blueprint by visiting several different Sunday morning church meetings. He did agree to have coffee a few times with Chuck, at the Village Eatery, and they enjoyed some lively conversations about life and faith and golf.

  The Sunday faith gathering that William liked best was the home church that Joe and Mitch and Simon attended. If he had chosen a local church he could call home, it would have been this one. They alternated venues each week and the meetings usually consisted of less than 20 people. He tried to get together with them once a month. He split his time among others in order to not ruffle any feathers by appearing magnetized toward anyone's faith persuasions or denominations, particularly since his beliefs did not fit the common mold. He knew that some believers would call him a strange bird, maybe not even in the flock.

  William avoided the heated political discussions that often occurred in the Village Eatery and other diners throughout the region. He refused to take the bait offered by those who had permanently camped on one side or the other, right or left, or those who had entrenched themselves in the middle. Not that he did not have preferences, but he had intentions of expressing a different style of persuasiveness on another topic. He would listen and nod as long as he could before discretely checking his watch and politely excusing himself. William hoped that by the end of his stay others would remember him for far more than his political ideology.

    Well into William's second month in town, a kind, older man, Phil, stopped by his table one Saturday morning to introduce himself as a close friend of Mitch's. For years Phil and Mitch had been fishing buddies and, in good weather or bad, they found enjoyment in hauling Phil's 14-foot, flat-bottomed fishing boat to various lakes hidden in the hills. Phil's small Johnson kicker on the transom eased them quietly along the grassy edges of pristine lakes as they tried to sneak up on, and sometimes catch, small-mouth bass, using a variety of lures. Their favorite was the purple worm with an iridescent tail.

    Most days, Phil wore a floppy fishing hat with some trophy flies fish-hooked on the brim, making him appear to be an experienced fly fisherman, but that was only a dream of his. He had recently moved well outside of town but still frequented the village and held his friendships together by regular house calls to his old friends. William expressed to Phil his love for fishing, and with that, their relationship took off. They spent some time angling, and occasionally they would even catch a fish. But more important was their growing camaraderie and the "fish stories" they brought back for all to hear at the Village Eatery.

Four Allies

William often called to mind those whom he considered to be his new allies and close friends who were being drawn into his strategies. To date they were; Joe, the one who worked at the hardware store and was the first to meet with him for breakfast; Mitch, the one with the beautiful family and the front porch facing Maine Street; Simon, the burly blind man with the well-trained Lab; and now Phil, a former pastor and the fisherman with dozens of entertaining tales of the outdoors in New Hampshire.

Of the four, Joe was the one William got to know best. They loved the game of baseball, had decent games of golf, liked driving four wheelers into rough terrain, loved their families and spoke openly to each other about their struggles in life. Joe acknowledged that his faith had been drawn early in his life toward the religious side where rituals and rules abounded. He knew there was more to spiritual life than just going to church, being good, and not dancing. Joe talked with William about how he had been on the lookout for a simple yet profound means for being changed for the better and loving neighbors. This was a setup for William.

    Joe came almost every Saturday morning to have breakfast at the table in the back corner, and the other three, Mitch, Simon and Phil, appeared often, as well, mainly due to Joe's vocal endorsement of William's credibility. Also, Wednesday night meetings had begun at William's small apartment including all five of them, using the five mugs purchased that second day at the farmhouse, a medium-sized table and five straight-backed chairs. Pizza was the only food item on Wednesday's dinner menu.

    By the third month, William received firm handshakes from most of the Saturday morning diners. He did not feel uncomfortable sitting at his own somewhat privatized table, because four allies regularly validated him by appearing soon after 7:30. Occasionally, one or two men outside of these four guys came by, and William would meet with them sometimes for hours, even it if meant being in the diner late into the evening. Friday or Saturday evening meetings were best for these other men, because it replaced their penchants for going off to places of vice. William always tipped generously for the food and extra coffees at these meetings, his way of appreciating Ritchie and the staff.

William stayed on course and remained discrete, not revealing too much of his plan, or why he had decided to come to this small New England village. In William's assessment, the stage was being set very nicely, and he remained a covert agent. It would have been easy at this point for some to assume that he was intending to do something on the clandestine side, perhaps not necessarily good for the people in town. But these doubts were usually harbored only briefly because William appeared to be such a genuinely nice guy.

The Plan

It wasn't until the first Saturday of the fourth month that the plan began to really escalate. Up until then, people had been reluctant to ask pressing questions. Yet, on this one Saturday, William observed two nearby patrons in the diner who were whispering, and he heard his name mentioned. They were bold enough to approach him at his back table. It finally came out as one of them said, "Hey William, what's up with the Wednesday night meetings at your apartment? Is it some kind of secret club or poker game?" William grinned and responded, "Those meetings help me stay on course and hold my ground in order to be right, to be ruled, and to be rich." They were even more puzzled and desperately wanted further information, but William closed it down by saying that he would talk about these three Rs in more detail soon, and other men would be invited to hear why they met on Wednesdays; now was not a good time. William was not worried because at least they had finally asked. On the inside, William was beaming with the possibilities of a big haul on his final Saturday in town.

William was known more and more for sitting in the diner on Friday and Saturday evenings with men whose lives were obviously in turmoil. His guests sat facing away from the other patrons in order to maintain discretion, even secrecy in their discussions. They would whisper softly to William as others passed by on their way to the restrooms. What was known by a few locals was that these men were in trouble with their family, their finances, their jobs, their addictions, or the law.

Locals would occasionally discuss the motorcycle accident, especially when Chris would drop by the diner to eat and talk with William on Friday or Saturday evenings. But those, who knew Chris well, thought, *What could be said by anyone to help him through such tragedies in his life?* Just as William had anticipated, there was increasing curiosity about his intentions in town. Some thought there was some type of subversive plot that was materializing. Others knew him better.

It was amazing how many people William had befriended by the time he had resided there for five months. Like his father before him, he never met a stranger. William knew it would be difficult and bizarre to suddenly leave town but that was the plan and his departure was now only one month away. Earlier this Saturday morning, at the back table, William told his four closest friends a spattering of details about the nature of his departure and the mission ahead. He asked them to keep it all under their hats until the time was right.

William's next to the last Saturday arrived, almost six months since he had driven into town, and everything was right on schedule. The proper people were in place for the grand finale breakfast. Some highly attentive people in town noticed that he was advertising in the newspaper the sale of his furnishings, and one lady at the electric company remembered the exact date that William wanted his power disconnected. The final billing coincided with next Saturday. William also announced a portion of his exit strategy confidentially to Chef Ritchie and the ladies.

Finally, he personally revealed to a few friends that he would host a free breakfast on his final Saturday morning in town. He said that he had to regrettably move to another venue. He expressed that he loved this region, but he was due to reside in another place soon. Ritchie, his staff and the four guys would all be in charge of handing out flyers that gave details of the fast approaching breakfast finale.

It was easy for some to speculate that his exit from this region could have something to do with William breaking the law, leading to some type of incarceration; or maybe he was heading into some medical facility. He instructed that it would be best if only men came on this final Saturday morning event, so there would be sufficient seating for those he had gotten to know best. The flyer read…

The Three Rs for Life
A Brief Presentation
by William Harris

"Be Right, Be Ruled, Be Rich"

This Saturday – 7:30 a.m.
At the Village Eatery
Breakfast is Free
For Men Only -Sign Up at the Counter
Curiosity, mainly about being rich and the

word "free," made the news spread quickly, and Ritchie ordered the needed ingredients necessary for the event. William gave Ritchie five hundred dollars in advance and said he would gladly give more if needed. They decided it would be a buffet, which would cut down on the workload of the waitresses. Ritchie's wife and family and staff fully committed to help in any way they could.

The last week, William made himself scarce in town in order to avoid too many probing questions. He knew that his carefully chosen words needed to be presented to all of them at one time, compassionately and adeptly, so he wrote and rewrote his post-breakfast speech.

On the final Wednesday at William's apartment, the guys required more pizza than ever, since the meeting would be long into the night. William made a quick visit to the pizzeria on the Tuesday before to order five super-large pizzas with varieties of toppings. The owners had heard about the Saturday morning event and wanted to come. "Sure thing. Guys only." William said. "Sign up at the diner. Breakfast is on me." The list of names on the clipboard at the Village Eatery check-out counter grew longer each day.

Friday evening William was sorting his many thoughts on how to deliver Saturday's speech, when Keith, a close friend who had worked a few odd jobs with William, rumbled up to his apartment on his classic Harley-look-a-like motorcycle. Keith had stood with William many times on the side of truth in their dialogues in town about man's purpose on earth. Together, they had painted, mowed, and hammered their way toward economic provision and always were ready to give an answer to others for the hope they had. Before riding off late that evening, Keith prayed with and for William and for the wisdom needed for the team to carry out their assignments at tomorrow's breakfast.

William still was apprehensive about how smoothly everything would go, particularly as he began to review not only what he would say but also how he would say it. William would need to emphasize early on that he wanted nothing from those who attended but only desired to give freely and offer them an opportunity to love a neighbor.

He had told the full plan to his team but had not done so to Ritchie because at the end of his speech, William would ask the attendees to consider putting a bill or two into the coffee can as they departed. He would explain this to them while Ritchie was being distracted by the servers in the kitchen. All of these funds would go for an exterior paint job on the diner, sprucing it up a little to help Ritchie's business. Most already would know that Ritchie had been battling cancer and was winning, but it had reduced his work hours and without his daily expertise, his business was down. Ritchie did not know the funds were for him and William, and the Wednesday night guys planned to tell him of the project on the front sidewalk after breakfast cleanup. Then and there, they would plan the events of the following week. With William gone, the guys would round up the materials needed for the paint job as well as some additional manpower from others in town. The paint project would take place the second Sunday afternoon after William left.

  By the time William tucked in on his last Friday evening in the village, it was past midnight. His bed frame, dresser drawers, favorite chairs, and many other items were already in the homes of others. He had little remaining except for the essentials he had brought with him six months earlier. His iPhone alarm was set for 5 a.m., and he had checked his Web site to make sure it was still active. If anyone wanted to know about the mystery of the three Rs, they could go there, anytime, and peruse his site.

  In each of the previous six month stays in other towns, he used a small diner like this one. In each place, William lived off of his Social Security, some monthly royalties from his writings, and whatever he could earn as a handyman. Each stay he made close friends, especially with four respected men in the community. With them in agreement, he began meeting in his apartment on Wednesday evenings for study and relationship building. Each time, he unobtrusively slipped into numerous local church services. Each time, he invited friends to meet with him at the back table of the diner, even beyond the Saturday morning slot. Each time, he offered the town to a free breakfast on his final Saturday. Each time, after the breakfast, he spoke briefly about the three R's and gave an opportunity for others to help toward a community need. And each time, he left a printed copy of what he had said for others to read or pass on. Always, a few would hang around after breakfast and talk with William and the four guys for a short while. William would leave a generous anonymous tip for the diner staff. He then moved on quickly to the next location without telling anyone exactly where he would be. William remained in regular contact through emails and his Web site with anyone who desired. There was always at least one who would step forward to continue hosting Saturday morning breakfasts.

Final Breakfast

At 7:00 a.m. the diner began to fill. The plan was to accommodate as many as possible and have those who could not squeeze in for the presentation and breakfast to come later that morning for their free breakfast. William had printed vouchers and paid Ritchie for them in advance.

By 7:50 all the breakfasts were on the tables in front of the hungry gathering. Stuffed mouths and the forks that rattled against the glass plates soon muffled the chatter. A little after 8 o'clock William stood, tapped his coffee cup, and thanked the staff for preparing the food and others for coming by for breakfast. He first told the short story of why he wore his black leather ball cap only on Saturdays. The floor and the audience were now his.

By 8:20 William finished his speech and breathed a deep sigh of relief. He reminded the attendees that others needed a table for breakfast so make the goodbyes short and don't forget the coffee can on the glass counter for helping a neighbor. Joe and Mitch would tally the giving side by side and see that it was properly applied to the project. All stood to exit the premises quickly and many headed toward William for a departing handshake. Those who wanted to help Ritchie placed a contribution in the coffee can. Some just left. Ritchie's son gave those who were waiting for tables a menu with the typed speech folded on the inside with a free voucher. A few printouts were placed near the register for anyone to read. The handout contained William's speech:

Good Morning,

    My name is William. Most of you have seen me around town working as a handyman or in the diner eating as a hungry man. This has been a terrific six months for me, thanks to so many of you, and though I do not want to leave, I must. My new residence will be far away to the south and I am not saying where so you will just have to stay in touch on my website.
    It was many years ago when a good friend of mine, in a small diner very much like this one, introduced me to the "Three Rs For Life" during our many meetings, some with breakfast and some with pizza. My life was forever changed thanks to him. Before I knew of these three R's, I was living outside of being right, being ruled and being rich, for I was usually wrong, unruly and poor.
    Some of you might think the three Rs stand for readin', writin', and 'rithmetic, and that would be a good guess, but not so. For your benefit, my four closest friends in town, Joe, Mitch, Simon,

and Phil have been meeting with me for some length of time in order to know well the same three Rs. Though I am leaving, these men will be available as qualified mentors of the Biblical truth of the three Rs.

The three Rs for life are:

>Be Right…
>Be Ruled…
>Be Rich…

I believe I know what some of you are thinking, for it was my first impression many years ago. First, you may be thinking, *he is going to tell me the things I need to do in order to be right.* Second, *he is going to swamp me with a boatload full of rules and regulations.* Or third, *here comes the latest pyramid scheme to make me rich.* But I will be speaking of none of those.

- First…be *Right* - "…*being found in Him, not having a righteousness of my own that comes from the law, but that which is through faith in Christ.*" Philippians 3:9

The truth is none of us can be right enough on

our own, we need help. Some say, get right. Some call it being righteous. But, we can only be in right standing with God when we accept his Son, Jesus Christ, for He became a perfect sacrifice for us, paying for our wrongs, our sins, by His death on the cross and bringing us new life through His resurrection.

- Second…be *Ruled* - *"For we know that our old self was crucified with him so that the body ruled by sin might be done away with, that we should no longer be slaves to sin."* Romans 6:6

In order to live on this earth with meaning, power and purpose, we must submit to godly rule. This is not living perfectly by every dictate of anyone's law, but living by the leading and power of Jesus Christ. When we submit to His will, believing in Christ and allowing Him to live His life through us, we are no longer ruled by selfishness and sin, for He has moved inside of us to offer His rule in and through us.

- Third…be *Rich* – *"I pray that the eyes of your*

heart may be enlightened in order that you may know the hope to which he has called you, the riches of his glorious inheritance inside his people." Ephesians 1:18

Too often, we hear rich defined as material wealth, but it is far above and beyond that. Being rich is to know God through faith in Jesus Christ for He is our worth, while on earth and forever beyond. He is our treasure inside of us, in jars of clay, and we can all be rich.

In conclusion, God does not force these "three Rs for life" upon anyone. He offers them freely and provides them when we truly believe and trust His Son, Jesus. Being *right* is the result of Christ moving on the inside of us by faith. Being *ruled* is humbly surrendering to the will and power of God with us. Being *rich* is knowing God as our abundance while on earth and in a promised heaven.

Today can be your day just like it was mine, many years back when my friend told me about these three Rs, for that was the day I chose Christ for Who He is. If you haven't already done so, will you choose Him today, turning away from old ways? …LONG PAUSE…

> For He is everything we need for life and godliness. – 2 Peter 1:3

Can we pray?

"Father, I pray that any who do not now know you for who you are, will accept your Son, Jesus, today. For He came to earth so we could be right, be ruled and be rich. All three come only by grace through faith in Jesus."

So be it…

Moving On

William stood for a long while afterward on the sidewalk in front of the diner as well-wishers said their goodbyes. Most dispersed within an hour, yet Joe, Mitch, Simon, and Phil, and four other men, Ritchie, Chuck, Chris, and Keith remained. At the right moment when quiet reflection appeared on each man's face, William removed his hat, bowed his head and prayed. The eight others did likewise. Richard, the proud owner of the hardware store, stood solemnly across the street carefully watching the men. Finally, all but Joe had departed.

Joe seemed to be the one most affected by William, his words and his life. Joe had lived in the village some time, all the while seeking Biblical truths where he could hang his hat. The three Rs were the truths he sought.

William slid behind the wheel of his truck just as Joe leaned in from the passenger side window saying, "Thank you for the mentoring. Some of us have already decided to continue the Saturday morning breakfasts at the back table and the Wednesday evening meetings with pizza. Godspeed William, no faster no slower. I'll be in touch."

As Joe Samuels walked away, down the sidewalk, he looked back and held up three fingers on his right hand for William to see in his rear view mirror. William reached his left arm out the window and returned the "Three R" salute and then eased away, considering his next assignment.

Although William would eventually go south, he first drove north up the winding blacktop road that went by the three-story farmhouse. The residence was still vacant, and he felt safe pulling off the road and into the driveway. He recalled the couple that had sold him the hat rack, the five coffee cups, some essentials, and the Boston Red Sox hat. He identified with their kind of melancholy brought about by having to leave their friends for a faraway land. He had been told by someone in town that the back porch of this farmhouse had been used for Sunday afternoon Gospel meetings, where a dozen or so believers would come for a meal prepared by the men, some songs led by a former police officer who brought his guitar, some Bible teachings and discussions and some prayer concluded with faithful agreement. William felt a kindred spirit with anyone who met for church in this fashion. As he peered a few paces up the other side of the road, he saw a faded white cross still firmly in place, holding its ground among the many gnarly weeds.

If for no other reason than Chris being present and attentive at that morning's breakfast, William felt it was worth his six-month stay. Chris seemed to be more firm in his understanding of hard times than when they first met at the cross on the side of the road six months prior. He was the first to come forward after William's speech and the first to ask if he could meet on Saturday mornings at the table in the back corner with whoever took his place. William smiled inside as he envisioned Chris on his Harley riding alongside Keith, learning about the narrow, winding, up-and-down roads of life and the treacherous turns.

The following Saturday morning, Ritchie asked one of the waitresses to add two more chairs around the back table. Joe Samuels welcomed and hosted five hungry men that morning.

For many years thereafter, the diner maintained its reputation for being a comfortable, friendly place where men could meet for a hardy Saturday morning breakfast, be who they really are, eat what they really like, sit and talk freely with close friends and not feel compelled to have to remove their ball caps while enjoying the best breakfast in the region. The table in the back of the Village Eatery held a place of honor for many men, for years to come.

Five years after moving to this small New Hampshire town, Joe and his wife had the opportunity to move abroad, living, working, and serving in faraway lands, often teaching conversationally the life-changing truth of the three Rs, be right, be ruled, be rich.

***Mentor**: ...one who influences a learning mind and a willing heart.*
urbandictionary.com – (emphasis mine)

A Father

Joey squeezed a hat-sized box into the overhead compartment before settling into his window seat for the 21-hour flight from central Nepal to the USA's east coast. Earlier that morning, on his brief Buddha Airlines flight from Pokhara to Kathmandu, Joey had made plans of how to challenge his dad to his recently devised contest, which he called "100 Ways Hats Help."

He was grateful to spend a few days with his mom and dad, since he was unable to visit often. Joey had served overseas for the past five years, not as a military soldier but as a teacher of English and an ambassador of Christ. He had booked a quick turnaround flight in order to be back to Nepal before the full force of the monsoon season hit the Himalayan foothills, where he and his wife lived for five months each year.

All the different ways that hats had helped him were on his mind as he tugged his favorite one, an ancient Red Sox ball cap, tightly onto his head. He pulled the brim downward, low enough to cover his eyes, for a power nap—at least until the flight attendants served the first round of snacks at 35,000 feet. Before he dozed off, he recalled the distinctive hats of the five men who had been so helpful during the formative stages in his life; a coach, a sage, an advocate, a mentor, and a father.

Joey was suddenly awakened by the rattling sound of a beverage cart jostling down the narrow aisle toward him. This meant that hot brewed instant coffee, some bottled water, and a sandwich with chips were on their way. But his better hope was to soon taste some southern-style sweet tea and egg salad sandwiches that his mom would have ready. His mouth watered as he remembered his mom's banana pudding. He thought to himself, *Do not forget the package in the overhead compartment.*

Joey, the name his father and mother still called him, had known for some time where he wanted this unique type of dialogue, about hats, to take place—in the family room of his childhood home in Central Florida where he and his sister had grown up under the loving tutelage of his parents, Martin and Elizabeth Samuels. Joey's plan was to categorize ball hats of his and his father's eras and how they helped them both in particularly unique situations. Mom would need to be present as well as narrator to keep the topics on track. She would probably have to confiscate the TV remote or Dad would remain glued to the news or sports channels. There should be plenty of fodder for discourse, since Joey's father had worn a vast array of hats in his many years of various types of employment. Joey was sure that his exceptional wit would allow him to interject many examples of how a hat had helped.

Also, Joey looked forward to this visit because his father had not been well. Martin in his 80s, was feeling the effects of congestive heart failure. It was a few years earlier in a conversation with Joey, that Martin had agreed with the apostle Paul in the book of Galatians, "that if man could be good enough for heaven on his own, then Christ died for nothing." Martin said on that occasion, "I believe Christ died for my sins and rose from the dead." That was pretty much the end of this type of discussion for him, since he did not like "religious talk." He believed it, and that settled it. Joey was confident of his father's impending entry into glory; Martin had said all along that the way to heaven must be simple or, as he saw it, "folk like me could not make it."

Joey had fine-tuned his writing skills while traveling overseas with his wife and considered someday scribing a screen play centered around this father-son game he was about to introduce. He envisioned the single stage setting to consist of an "All in the Family" style living room, with the father in his favorite recliner near the TV, a mother crocheting in her rocker, and a son involved in speaking up on issues that stirred his dad's sensibilities. But, in this case, if father and son stayed on the topic of how hats help, interesting family history would be unveiled.

After his 15-hour-flight, from Dubai to Orlando, Joey hailed a taxi and was able to catch a 30-minute power nap on his way home. As quietly as possible, he entered the family homestead, since Joey felt confident that this was still the common ingress and egress of the home on the corner of Helen and Spruce. The door needed only a simple tap and a request for entry from a familiar voice for Martin or Elizabeth to say, "Come on in."

"Hello! Anyone alive in here?" Joey called.

"Just barely," Dad answered. "Come in this house. Let me see you. Glad you made it."

"Me too. Where's Mom?

"You know the answer to that. She's in the kitchen, making something special for her two favorite men."

"Hey Mom!" Joey exclaimed. "You look great! I see you are in your private culinary domain."

"Yup. This is me," she said. "Good to see you, Son. I've missed you and love you. Would you care for some iced tea?"

"Of course. I love you, too, Mom. You are the best."

"Your father has really been looking forward to spending some time with you."

"And me with him."

Joey turned to his father, "You look good, Dad. I hope you're feeling better."

"No complaints, Son, as if they would do any good anyway. I still have a good appetite, I can cruise a block or two each morning provided I take along my seven iron as a walking stick, and your mom keeps an eye out for me."

"She always has," Joey said.

"How about you, Son? How's everything going for you overseas? Are you still preaching to the poor in remote villages and is your wife still involved with the Children's Home?"

For the next hour, Joey brought Dad up to speed, particularly on his adventures in Nepal and his rough, four-wheeling jaunts into small mountain villages. Also, he assured his dad that his wife, Ann, was firmly by his side, the woman he deeply loved, respected, and needed.

"You know Dad, it's because of you that I have pursued such adventurous goals. You always believed in me, even back when you let me drive that 13-foot Crosby boat with the 75 horsepower Johnson bolted to the back. Up and down the river I went, but I knew you were always covering my back.

"If you say so. But wasn't there a time when you ran it high and dry when you missed a turn in the Oklawaha River?"

"Sure was," Joey agreed, "But you came along soon and shoved the fiberglass boat off the protruding cypress knees, changed the cotter pin and confidently pointed me upstream, toward Silver Springs."

Joey sensed it was time to get onto the topic of hats and the 100 ways a hat can help a man, so, he explained to his father that he had come up with a way to recall some of their great times together centering around the topic of ball hats.

"Sounds interesting," Dad said. "I'll do my best to stir the grey matter, since a bit of fog may have settled in."

But before the hat challenge began, Joey started off by mentioning the farm his father was raised on in Kentucky.

"I remember that your family's farm was in Adairville, Kentucky, before the Great Depression of 1929, right?" Joey stated as a question.

"Yep," his dad confirmed. "We were tobacco farmers. As for ball caps, they were rare. But, if any, they were worn by tractor mechanics and feed salesmen. Myself, I usually settled for anything that would keep my head and ears protected from the elements."

"You delivered ice blocks door-to-door from the back of a cooler truck, didn't you?" Joey continued.

"Yep, that's how I met your mom. I made a dollar a day. I think I had an old corduroy ball hat that I would stuff my gloves into before I collected and counted the coins on the front porch railings."

"Didn't Mom live across the state line, in Barren Plains, Tennessee?"

"Yep, and she was as pretty as an angel. Her dad, Papa, was always watching me like a hawk when I walked to their front door, ice in tow, hooked by that fierce looking twin forked pick. After a while, I think your mom started peeking through the front curtains, looking for me to drive up on Saturday mornings. I know I was always looking forward to seeing her."

Just then, Mom came in with the sweet tea on ice. She had been listening from the kitchen, evidenced by her blushing face.

"I know that it's hard for you to talk about the war, Dad, but can we for a moment?"

"A little."

"I guess the best hat you could have back then," Joey posed, "was a standard combat issue Army helmet.

"Yep. It saved my life a few times. But many in my battalion were lost. What made it even harder was that, back then, soldiers were put into units, where they were all from the same town or county. So, when someone died in battle next to you, it was like losing a best friend or a brother that you grew up with."

"Do you still have a soft spot in your heart for Fords? I remember the '51 in the side yard with the shifter on the column. I learned to drive in that car, or at least rev the engine and pretend shifting the gears."

"My love for Fords began when I worked at Summers Ford in Springfield as the service manager. Wearing that dealership hat in our local town meant a great deal to me. The sales team sold a lot of cars because the customers knew they would be taken care of by my department if they had a mechanical problem. The hat would get greasy from being under the car lift rack. A dirty hat meant you worked hard. Your mom was proud of my hard work. It paid the bills for the four of us. But, my favorite cap was the one with a shiny black brim and 'Ford' embroidered on the crest. It was my Sunday-drivin' hat."

"I remember that hat," Joey said. "I also remember we moved to Ocala in the early 50s so you and your best friend could own and operate a truck stop."

"Yep. I think I had a Shell Oil hat back then. We pumped a lot of gas in that location until the main highway bypassed us. We got into financial trouble quickly. I had to find other work."

Joey asked, "Is that when you became a long-haul trucker?"

"Yep," said his dad. "I drove a GMC tractor that pulled a refrigerated trailer from Orlando to New York City, loaded to the gills with boxes of orange concentrate. I usually had to dead-head back."

"After you stopped at the loading dock in NYC, I remember how I was small enough to crawl up into the trailer on my belly, on top of the cardboard containers to give you the count."

"Alterman Trucking was my work hat for many years. I remember putting a rock on the accelerator as my cruise control so I could get the cramp out of my right leg."

After a brief bathroom break, Joey came back through the kitchen, where mom was putting the final touches on the egg salad with just the right amount of mayonnaise and relish, chopped boiled eggs, pinches of salt and pepper and a slight squeeze of mustard. She set their meals on TV trays in front of each of them before she slipped away. Joey was glad that she gave them some more time to talk.

All Joey said was "boats" and his dad quickly continued.

"First it was Bob's Boats and Motors, where I worked as a salesman and boat rigger. My friend, the owner, gave me a chance, and I learned to love the boating and fishing scene in Florida.

"So, you took the plunge," Joey said.

"Yep, and almost drowned. I bought a marine dealership in a landlocked area of Kissimmee. I was loyal and wore a Johnson Outboard hat, although Mercury seemed to be most people's favorite, at least for speed."

Joey added, "I remember those early Saturday morning one-hour drives with you so I could work at the dealership with you. I would sweep the floors, clean the bathrooms, rig boats and occasionally get to test drive a new boat on Lake Toho."

"I think you wore a Gator hat about that time. Do you remember driving to Jacksonville and picking up those Gator boat trailers, stacking them six high behind your '57 Chevy?"

"Yes. Those were my truckin' days. And, I remember the guys in the office giving me an extra Gator sticker that I put on the back windshield of that same '57 Chevy, the one you gave me on my 16th birthday. Some of my old high school friends still call me "Gator." I may have chosen the University of Florida as my first college because of that."

"Those were great days. I bet you had no idea just how broke we were then."

"How can you say 'broke?' We always had good food on the table, a roof over our heads and some classic cars and boats at our fingertips. Mom custom made madras shirts, and we piled into a new and different boat almost every weekend, taking trips up the St. Johns River, or winding our way through the Butler Chain in Windemere or heading down the Kissimmee River.

"I often tell the story of how I slalomed behind a 17-foot Cobia cabin cruiser, powered by a 75-horsepower Johnson Outboard all the way from the St. John's River Bridge, near Sanford, to Ponce de Leon Springs, non-stop. It must have been 35 miles."

"If it was an inch," Dad laughed. "You remember?"

"How could I ever forget? I would have drowned at the end but for that tiny foam waist belt they called a life preserver. I was numb all over, and you and mom and sis had to drag me into the boat before the gators headed our way from the banks. How about your next hat?"

"This one was a little tougher to wear. When we had to let go of Central Marine Sales, your mom and I did what we had to do to survive. First, it was sub-contracting some home construction in Orlando, partnering with a good friend of mine. I wore a builders supply hat and a t-shirt when I was supervising construction and a white collared shirt and no hat when I was in the sales office.

"Yeah, we lived in one of those homes you built. You made it very affordable, and it was a beautiful two-story model home on the west end of town. I was into Corvettes and making money about this time and kind of lost my way."

Martin made no comment but only graciously paused and reached for another sip of sweet tea.

"Next for me was what you might call fruit and vegetable entrepreneurship. You remember. The hat I mostly wore said Indian River Fruit. That was the special brand that your mom and I packed into the automobile trunks of tourists who were headed north after visiting Disney World. It felt like farming again, before sunup until after sundown. I should have had a ball hat embroidered that said, 'Orange Shack,'" Dad laughed.

"About then," said Joey, "I was changing my means of livelihood—something that was very painful—but it needed to be done. You helped me land on my feet by giving me a chance to work with you peddling some of your oranges at the front corner of a gas station. I remember that at age 60 you could hoist those two-bushel, hundred-pound boxes to the third tier of your old pickup. They were so high that the truck would wobble with the least crosswind as you crawled down the two-lane highway from Merritt Island to Orlando. I know that Mom's shoulders are aching today because of her laboring beside you."

"It pains me to think of it," said Dad.

"Didn't you have a motorhome about then?"

"Yep. She was old, but she was a beauty and big enough to give us a place to rest behind the Orange Shack. Later, we had some other motorhomes, too. I guess I was also in the real estate business for a while, developing some land I came across near Disney, but that's another story."

"I'm proud of you, Dad. You are amazing to me. You and Mom are both inspiring. She was just who you needed. Dare I mention golf without you going for the TV clicker?"

"I loved it and still do, but now I just watch it on the tube, especially the back-nine finish of the Masters. You and your sons made golf so fun for me, either when we played together, or when I could walk along the edge of the fairway to watch. I see that you are wearing a Titleist hat."

"Yeah. I have an 8 a.m. tee time tomorrow at Dubsdread Country Club with three of my old high school friends. It's a quick reunion since I have to return to Nepal in a few days. Wanna tag along?"

"Surely not to Nepal and not this time on the course. Tell them I said, 'Hey!' Play the game as long as you can, Son. Do you remember Maggie Valley?"

"Yes, I do. I loved those times you and mom drove all the way to North Carolina to watch the junior golf events that I had organized as a golf coach. Golf sure took a load off of my mind in those days. I was wearing a Red Bird golf hat about that time."

Mom was in her element as she came in with the dessert, banana pudding with vanilla wafers—her signal that it was time to shift to the "Hats That Help" challenge.

"Here is how we will do this hat contest," Joey said. "We will alternate answers. I will mention one way a ball cap can help, and then you will say another. We will try to reach 100 within a few minutes, and then we get a second helping of banana pudding. Any questions?"

"I think I understand," answered Dad. "Can you give me a clue on the first one?"

"Sure. I'll go first. To help shield your temple from a dangerously wayward golf ball."

"To help put out a fire, the one you started by trying to cook anything in oil in the kitchen," Dad laughed.

"To help keep your head protected from the baking sun or the frigid air," Joey continued as the two men went back and forth.

"To help muffle or conceal an emotion."

"To help stop sweat from running down into your eyes."

"To help put in plain sight a gun logo to ward off any perpetrators."

"To help swat with and fend off a rabid animal."

"To help shield your eyes from the late afternoon sun on a par 5 finishing hole as you examine your second shot possibilities."

"To help hide your money clip and wrist watch on top of your head as you walk through a bad section of town."

"To help hold up as a shield for your eyes as the sun glares off the lake while you pull the kids around on water skies."

Mom chimed in, "That's 10. Any thoughts?"

"Dad, you never were much of a cook, at least indoors," Joey said.

"Yeah, but an iron skillet over an open fire on the bank of the St. Johns River with some eggs tells a different story," retorted Dad.

Mom continued, "Now, on to number eleven and beyond. How about the category of how a hat can help to honor others?"

"By tipping your ball cap when introducing yourself to a lady."

"By removing your cap as the National Anthem is played."

"By taking off your hat in church or as someone prays."

"As taught in the military, by uncovering anytime you enter a building."

"For waving to the crowd from the top of the dugout steps after a home run."

"For a gallant sweep before a princess or a queen."

"To acknowledge the crowd from a convertible at your homecoming parade."

"To tap honorably from the brim as you address the elderly."

"To congratulate a job well done by acknowledging, 'Hats off to you.'"

"To hold an emblem for identifying with those who have been in harms way in defense of liberty."

Mom interjected again. "That's 20. Any more thoughts?"

"I guess I should have mentioned giving honor to vets in a Veteran's Day Parade," Dad said.

"Yep; me too," Joey added.

"The next category is about appearance," Mom explained. "And we may go for 20 on this one."

Joey began, "Helps to make you appear taller."

"Helps to make you look younger," Dad smiled.

"Helps to make you look older," Joey winked.

"Helps to cover baldness."

"Helps to have a place to hide your long hair, especially on the weekends when you have Army Reserve drill.

"Helps to make a long nose look shorter."

"Helps to change your appearance quickly from a formal shirt and tie to a casual look, like a politician at a small town rally.

"Helps to let people know who you are rooting for at the Daytona 500."

"Helps to give a goofy look as you tilt sideways for a quick laugh."

"Time out!" Dad interrupted as he turned his hat 45 degrees and scrunched his nose. "Do you mean like this?"

"That's the goofy look, alright," Joey agreed.

"To help lead a baseball rally by turning it around backwards."

"To help scoop minnows for bass fishing."

"To help cover the worry wrinkles in your forehead."

"To help in being recognized as one of the good old boys even though you've never slaughtered a pig."

"To help cover a bad hair day."

"To help you hide your chewing gum in a fancy restaurant."

"To help say you have been to that part of the world."

"To help you just plain look better than in your usual dull, hatless state."

"To help disguise the stigma of wearing eyeglasses or hearing aids."

"To help you look like a hard worker as you tilt it back from your forehead and wipe imaginary sweat from your brow."

"To let your wife know you are headed for the golf course."

"OK, guys," Mom said. "Good job! That's a total of 40. Any words?"

"Lets move on," Dad replied. "I need some dessert."

"The next category is practical," Mom continued. "Your son thinks that this can have as many as 50."

"Oh, time out!" Dad exclaimed. "Fifty is a stretch."

"Come on, Dad," Joey said. "I've never known you to quit at anything. I'll start: to help become a manly hero by capturing a small critter scurrying across the floor."

"To help in scooping some drinking water out of a cool Colorado stream," Dad said.

"To help catch or deflect a deviously thrown snowball," Joey said.

"To help seize a homerun ball from the bleachers, robbing it from the tall guy in front of you with the expensive glove," Dad laughed.

"Yep," Joey laughed, too. "And to help knock the dirt off your shoes before you enter the house."

"To help keep the grease out of your hair and off your eyebrows, since you had spent most of the day working beneath a broken down car."

"To help cover your face and use for deep breathing into in order to stop hyperventilation."

"To help desperately fan oxygen into a dying flame at the BBQ grill you're in charge of on Thanksgiving."

"To help hide your ponytail in a business meeting."

"To help keep your dandruff from falling onto your dark shirt collar."

"To help keep your contact lenses from being blown out of your eyes in a strong wind in the desert."

"To help gather warm water from the radiator of your Army jeep for washing your face and shaving."

"To help check for bad breath before your big date," Joey quipped. The two men laughed, and Dad continued.

"To help filter coffee grounds when you are in the middle of nowhere and in desperate need of caffeine."

"To help take a quick splash shower before a night out at the bowling alley."

"To help collect paper ballots at an impromptu election."

"To help gather berries from a country field for a surprise picnic treat for your gal."

"To help muffle screams when you have had all you can handle."

"To indicate that you are entering the fray of a political contest by tossing it into the ring."

"To help take up a quick offering for the less fortunate men who fought in the war and still fight the memories."

"To help you cover your face as you nap in the airport, during a long layover, or snooze on the couch at home, or take a siesta on a park bench."

"To help cover your young son's face, blocking the bright sun as he tries to sleep next to you on the long overnight drive home."

"To help scrape the New Hampshire ice off the windshield with its already frozen bill."

"To help in swatting away the flies and other bothersome insects from the picnic table."

"To help hold onto your best thoughts during a long walk in the woods."

"To help you with self-esteem, since it is not fickle; it always fits no matter your body size."

"To hold a company logo that will make you wealthy when you've just won a PGA event on live TV."

"To help shield your glasses from the raindrops that could blur your vision as you play golf in a hurricane."

"To help cool your head as you throw it to the ground when you've lost it over a bad call against your son on the ball field."

"To help as a gauge for true horizontal when you try to read the slope of a green."

"Only 30 more," Joey says. "You're doing great, Dad. Here's another one: to help get the umpire's attention as you brush off home plate in order to give him a clue."

"To help wave a kid home from the third base coaching box," Dad adds.

"To toss in the air as you identify with a graduating class from a trade school."

"To have something meaningful to give as a trophy to the kids who made the Little League team."

"To use as a pot holder so you don't burn your hand as you remove a pot of burned spaghetti sauce from the stove top."

"To help hide the marbles from Grandma that you won under the big oak tree during recess."

"To illustrate secrecy when you remove it and gesture to a friend, 'Keep it under your hat.'"

"To locate a high fly as you flip your sunglasses in place as the sun glares down or the night lights are turned on at the baseball field.

"To help hold your reading glasses on top of your head when they are not in use."

"To help secure a golf tee close to your ear since you are always forgetting where you put it."

"To help hold a magnetic ball marker on the expensive golf hat you bought at Shinnecock Hills during the U.S. Open in Long Island."

"To help in waving for attention and signaling for emergency aid whenever in any kind of trouble."

"To help remind drivers that while you are under the bright orange one, you are jogging on the side of the road."

"To help carry eggs to the farmhouse from the chicken coop."

"To help 'fit in' at a local breakfast diner that may be anywhere in small town America."

"To help hold your keys and small personal belongings on the bureau after a long, exhausting day."

"To help fan the air in the direction of your gal in order to keep her from perspiring."

"To help show you are one of only a few who was recently chosen to play in an official Little League baseball game."

"To help stop a hockey puck from knocking out someone's teeth.

"To help let your wife know that the workday is done when you hang it on the bedpost at night."

Mom interrupted. "I know you could go on, but let's stop at 50 on that category. So, think for a moment about the final 10. Any category will do."

Well," mused Dad, "From our list so far, I don't know how any man can be a man without a good ball cap."

"I'm with you on that, Dad," Joey agreed.

"Are you ready?" Mom asked. "OK, ten more and we can have dessert. This is an open category. Ready, Go!"

Joey began, "To show others that you are a real player by proudly displaying the downward-turned brim, like your dad or coach taught you when you were just a rookie."

"To preserve fond memories every time you walk by the hat rack in the garage."

"To have it ready for a celebrity to quickly sign as a souvenir while others are fumbling for their program."

"To let everyone know that you are a true fan, even though your team never seems to win."

"To make a fashion statement when you find one that matches your T-shirt color."

"To protect your head from the elements when you walk your dog, rain or shine."

"To remind you of how much better things used to be, back in the day.'

"To show respect at the end of a golf match by removing it and shaking hands with opponents and their caddies, win or lose."

"To tuck your gloves in as you collect and count the coins for the block of ice that you brought to farm houses.

"OK, time out," said Joey. "The final one is yours, Dad."

Mom and Joey paused respectfully until Dad had gathered his wits. Joey knew his wisdom and years of experience would rule the day.

"Number 100," Dad proclaimed, "is to have a covering to pull firmly on your head and wiggle from side to side as you express with determination that what lies ahead will be very difficult."

Joey knew his father had done it; here was a philosophy of life spoken with the tug and wiggle of a hat, even if there were no accompanying words. That poignant gesture is representative of what many consider to be a bygone era and how much better could it be said that we need to take life head on, with resolve of character and sheer determination in order to best do what is next.

"That's 100," Mom said. "How did you do that? It took just less than 20 minutes! You guys are amazing!"

"That was great," Joey agreed. "Who won?"

"Ah, it was a tie," said Dad. "Fifty-fifty. Now, are we going to keep on blubbering about this, or did somebody say something about some banana pudding?"

"It'll be ready in a minute," Mom laughed. "Goodness gracious guys."

Joey sneaked out to the garage and retrieved the box that had flown with him in the overhead compartment. His dad looked puzzled. Joey gave him the gift and waited as he removed the duct tape wrapping. Martin immediately lit up, just as Joey had expected. He wondered if his father could have worn this very same hat back in the late 40s as he cruised around in a shiny new Ford. It was perfect. The cloth top of the hat was beige colored and had the Ford emblem sewn into its crest, with a firm glossy black rounded bill protruding in a semi-circle on the front. The hat was advertised on Amazon and was popular just about the time that his father had worked at the Ford dealership in Springfield, Tennessee."

"Where in the world did you find this?" Martin asked. "What a treat. Thanks, Son; I'm glad to have a 'Sunday drivin' hat again."

"You're more than welcome, Dad. You can find almost anything online these days. I thought you would like it. Does it still have some grease on the brim?"

"You know; I think it does. Smells like it could have come from an open coffee can in the back shop in Springfield."

With moisture building up in his eyes, Joey had trouble taking a photo but gave a quick click as Dad tried on his latest collectible. Shortly, they finished dessert and gave their goodbye hugs until the next day, when Joey would report back on his round of golf.

As Joey exited, he glanced over his shoulder just in time to see his father positioning his new gift—an old Ford hat—firmly onto his head and wiggling it briefly from side to side into a tighter position. He had that determined clinch in his jaw, and his sparkling eyes squinted slightly. This was the same expression that Joey had seen so many times, just before his father headed into the stormy headwinds of life. His father's mannerisms reminded Joey of number 100, just as he believed his father had intended them to do.

Later in the week, on his long, three-stage return flight to Dubai, then Kathmandu, then Pokhara, Joey centered his thoughts around five eras in his life when a man fitted with a distinct hat entered his life and gave of himself for his well-being. He realized that the proof of their profound impact on him was that he had replicated them and their style somewhat in his own life, as he too became for others a coach, a sage, an advocate, a mentor, and a father. Coach and sage had passed on, but Joey was glad to still be in touch with the advocate and the mentor. Before long, Martin, his father, would slip into a glorious heavenly home his Eternal Father had prepared for him.

Joseph Robert Samuels hoped he had lived a stellar life, such that others he knew would want to imitate, in their own unique ways, the best of him as they faced challenges in life akin to his.

It was during the coach and sage era that Joseph discovered the proverbial calling to higher ground written of in the Bible: *"The noble man makes noble plans, and in noble deeds he stands."*

From the advocate he learned to be tougher and more resilient, even confrontational when necessary, to hold fast to truth and look for high ground in the unsettling times.

While alongside the mentor he discovered the simple yet profound foundation of his Christian faith, one he learned to live by and could easily verbalize with others; be right, be ruled and be rich.

As for his father, Joey loved him, and was very proud of him, but it was only after Martin's death that Joey got to know and love him even more by conversing with others who knew his dad better than he did. His father was a dreamer but possessed staunch determinism that brought to reality many imaginings. His even-tempered manner, ever-present wit, kindness and inherent wisdom were most distinct. He was an unsung, courageous American hero and a man of many hats that were suitable for the current need and often had to be obligingly worn. He was a father who was perfectly fit for Joey.

Five men, a coach, a sage, an advocate, a mentor and a father were for Joey, J.R., Joseph, Joe, and Joey, God's manly grace personified.

***Father**- "A man who raises, loves and protects his children, strives to be a worthy role model and always wants the best for them now and eternally beyond." JRS

Made in United States
Orlando, FL
09 April 2024